Reviews of H.N. Hirsch's previous Bob & Marcus
mysteries, *Shade*, *Fault Line* & *Rain*

From N. N. Light's Book Heaven

If you love courtroom drama and murder mystery, you'll be drawn in with *Rain*. My Rating: 5 stars

A murder among the elite puts Bob and Marcus in a game of cat and mouse most deadly. *Rain* is a classic courtroom mystery even Perry Mason would applaud. Every detail of the investigation and trial is expressed through narration, action, and intriguing characters. This mystery will captivate readers until the very last page. The foreshadowing is subtle yet brilliant.

The mystery itself is well-plotted—the tension is taut—the reader is thrown into the investigation. The ending caught me by surprise. A brain teaser leaving the reader wanting more. Well done.

From Oberlin Prof. Emerita Sandra Zagarell

Shade, Fault Line, and now *Rain*. If you're not yet a fan of H.N. Hirsch's "Marcus and Bob Mystery" series, you should be. These smart, accomplished, and very believable men, who become a couple in *Shade*, combine their skills and knowledge, Marcus as a college professor and Bob as a lawyer, as they untangle the webs of intrigue that surround murder.

Each book engages with major contemporary issues: the toxic culture of an elite university, the corruption of political ambition, the sleaziness of the sex-for-hire economy. All three books feature terrific writing and great pacing along with accomplished characterization. Hirsch deftly develops Marcus and Bob's domestic and emotional life as both separate from and enmeshed in their sleuthing, and he weaves in their relationships with their friends, Bob's family, their colleagues, and various unsavory academics, politicians, and lawyers.

... Bob decides to defend Marcus's graduate student Kenny against the charge of having murdered his girlfriend Cathy, an acting student, and Marcus and Bob—and we—keep trying to figure out what's a performance and what isn't. Bob has to wrestle with ethical problems to which there are no clear solutions, and *Rain* ends on a cliffhanger which poses questions about justice.

—Sandra A. Zagarell,
Donald R. Longman Professor of English Emerita at Oberlin College

Hirsch weaves his tale well, capturing Southern California ambience and the interplay of his characters cinematically.

—Grady Harp of Goodreads

Fault Line is a suspenseful and utterly gritty crime fiction book. . . . Thoroughly satisfying.   —the Onlinebookclub.com

Written in the classic style of James Ellroy, *Fault Line* is a murder mystery you won't soon forget. With a full cast of characters, a scenic setting, plus a laundry list of suspects, I couldn't stop reading until the dramatic conclusion. Fans of *L.A. Confidential* will enjoy this political murder mystery. 5+ stars!   —N. N. Light's Book Heaven

Libraries and readers looking for a classic gay murder mystery steeped in California culture, political subterfuge, and characters that live on the line of lies and danger will find *Fault Line* a fine study in intrigue . . . packed with social and political as well as psychological and relationship insights. Hirsch brings to life a myriad of characters that swirl around this unique murder case and its accompanying special interests. A memorable, compelling read. . . .

— Diane Donovan, *Midwest Book Review*, Donovan's Bookshelf

Bob and Marcus are a gay Nick and Nora, a couple you'll want to spend time and solve mysteries with.

—Jean Redmann, author of
the award-winning Micky Knight Mystery Series

I loved *Shade* and wondered if author H. N. Hirsh could meet the same high standard. I shouldn't have worried. *Fault Line* was just as good, and just as fresh. This time we're immersed in law and politics in California, as Bob, now a lawyer, has to figure out the twists and turns of ambition, corruption, and secrets that result in a murder and authorities' resistance to discovering the perpetrator. Well-written and engrossing, *Fault Line* is a must-read for everyone who loves thrillers.

—"SMZ" on Amazon

"The Thin Man" goes to Harvard! This is a remarkable first novel which I read in one sitting. Good stuff. A young assistant professor buffeted about by the whims of senior colleagues in the Harvard Government Department circa the 1980s finds redemption and adventure in the midst of murder and scandal in Maine and Massachusetts. The gay romance part reminds me of the old 1930s *Thin Man* films.

—Michael A. Mosher on Amazon

Shade is part murder mystery, part romance novel, part travelogue, and a delight to read. Murder is gruesome business, especially when it involves a young man in the prime of life, but Hirsch excels in tempering harsh reality with pleasant characters, summertime on the New England coast, academic intrigue and, perhaps best of all, a charming tale of two people falling in love.

—Anthony Bidulka, author of
the Merry Bell P.I. trilogy and *Going to Beautiful*
winner of Crime Writers of Canada Best Crime Novel

Move over. Bob is driving! Hirsch's second mystery (*Fault Line*) is better than his first! Keep them coming! —KB on Amazon

A jolly good murder mystery, stylishly rendered with a swift-moving plot and loads of local color. Fans of the British murder mystery and LGBTQ romance/mystery genres will find much to savor here. I devoured it in a single session while flying across the Atlantic, passing the time much more enjoyably than with the airline's on-board entertainment!

—Wayne A. Cornelius on Amazon

Fun & intelligent! I love keeping up with this couple, and I learn something new with every mystery they solve. —Linda S. on Amazon

A fabulous gripping mystery, plus a love story. A terrific read! I have become very fond of Bob and Marcus (from the first book in this series, *Shade*). Just as they arrive in San Diego Bob is dragged into a murder investigation. There's all kinds of intrigue and plot twists, and, in the process, a vivid portrayal of San Diego, both gay and straight. Well narrated, great characters! Kept me turning pages to discover who done it. —Priscilla Long on Amazon

In *Shade*, Hirsch writes beautifully and immediately draws you into a world of Harvard, old money, gay romance, and murder most foul. The narrative drives forward almost effortlessly, and is punctuated by one plot twist after another. Can't wait for the next book in the series!

—KB on Amazon

Could not put it down! I am not a regular reader of mysteries. Yet, when I picked up this book, I could not put it down. The author's attention to detail, familiarity with the southern California setting, and knowledge about law & police investigations held my attention and kept me guessing about the identity of the murderer. . . Highly recommended.

—CE Smith on Amazon

Pisgah Press was established in 2011 to publish and promote works of quality offering original ideas and insight into the human condition and the world around us.

Published by Pisgah Press, LLC
PO Box 9663, Asheville, NC 28815
www.pisgahpress.com

Book & design: A. D. Reed, MyOwnEditor.com

This is a work of fiction. All the characters and events portrayed in this book are either products of the author's imagination or are used fictitiously.

Library of Congress Cataloging-in-Publication Data
Winter/H.N. Hirsch

ISBN-13: 978-1-942016-96-0
First Edition
June 2025
Printed in the United States of America

Winter

H. N. Hirsch

Pisgah Press
Asheville, NC

What good is the warmth of summer, without the cold of winter to give it sweetness.

— John Steinbeck

Winter

Bob didn't cry at the funeral. Marcus didn't notice, crying buckets himself. Their daughter stood between them, holding their hands.

All three of them remembered that moment for a long time. Lily especially remembered looking up at the mountains in the distance, seeing snow on the peaks. It had been an unusually cold December despite the California sun, and they were bundled up in sweaters and jackets, noses running.

1

Bob had always thought his mother would die first, after her harrowing battle with cancer ten years before; he had even said as much to Marcus, who agreed. But Ruth pulled through. The cancer never returned, and the whole ordeal made her more cheerful than she had ever been, which was saying something.

They were both thrilled when, a year after Ruth's last radiation treatment, she and Bob's father, Jake, decided to retire to Laguna Beach, halfway between San Diego, where they lived, and Los Angeles, where Bob's brother Alex and his family had settled years before. Marcus always marveled at how well they all got along; he felt much closer to Bob's family than his own chilly, distant brood in Chicago. With their adopted daughter Lily and Alex and Carol's two children, Marcus felt part of something, something he never had growing up, and he loved the occasions when they all got together. Bob sometimes grumbled about the traffic when they drove to Laguna or LA for this or that, but Marcus always made him smile again by suggesting they play twenty questions or sing a silly song, which Lily loved. She had a lovely voice and was interested in music. And Lily adored her grandparents and aunt, uncle, and cousins.

Then, out of nowhere, Jake had a heart attack. After being stabilized at the local hospital he was airlifted to UCLA for surgery but was gone by the time the helicopter landed. They were never sure exactly what had happened; in keeping with Jewish tradition, they declined an autopsy. That was contrary to California law, since the exact cause of death was unclear, but somehow Alex, a well-connected lawyer, finagled it; he had gone to the hospital to meet the helicopter.

Bob heard the news over the phone from Alex's wife, Carol, always the steadiest presence among them—"a rock," according to her husband. Marcus long remembered watching the color drain from Bob's face as he held the kitchen phone to his ear, and knew what had happened before hearing Bob say it. They had learned of the heart attack earlier in the day and both rushed home from work, where they paced around the house, wondering what they could do, realizing that there was nothing but to wait for the phone to ring.

After he got off the phone, Bob said nothing. Marcus hugged him, and Bob went out to the back yard, where Lily was playing with their golden retriever, Zelda. He crouched down to tell Lily what had happened, and though she didn't cry, she hugged Bob for a long time. They sat on the grass as the sun started to set and Zelda, sensing something was wrong, laid her head on Bob's lap. Finally the cool air drove them back inside, where Marcus threw together dinner that none of them had an appetite for. Bob drank nearly a whole bottle of wine, but he was up early the next morning to drive up to Laguna Beach to be with his mother. Marcus and Lily drove up that evening. No one spoke much—there was nothing to say.

The graveside funeral was held the next day, a simple ceremony officiated by the rabbi from the Orange County congregation Jake and Ruth had joined when they arrived. A few family friends from Connecticut flew cross-country to be there, people Bob remembered from growing up, including his father's long-time legal secretary, whom he had adored as a boy. It was startling to see all of them suddenly appear in California and see how they had aged. Bob was already feeling old, since he was about to turn forty—the visitors brought his age even closer to home.

They held an open house that evening, but they would not sit shiva—the traditional Jewish week of mourning. Bob was in the middle of a trial, Marcus was finishing his Fall quarter of teaching, and Alex had to get back to his new, struggling law firm. The kids would be better off back in school, they all thought.

"I'll be fine," Ruth assured them. "Go back to your lives. Take care of the kids. That's what he would have wanted."

No one really believed she was fine, or thought she should be alone, but everyone nodded. She sent them all home with piles of food that friends and neighbors had dropped off, casseroles and cakes and baskets of fruit. Bob and Marcus drove back to San Diego with Lily and Jay, their nineteen-year-old nephew, a sophomore at UC San Diego where Marcus was on the faculty. Lily fell asleep in the back seat with her head on Jay's lap. Seeing the cousins in the rearview mirror, Marcus felt something move inside of him.

They dropped Jay off on campus, collected Zelda from the neighbor who was watching her, and then drove home and put Lily to bed. Bob took a bath, nursing a tall glass of scotch.

2

The next few weeks were hard to remember. They both forced themselves to concentrate on work, Bob defending a client he didn't like against a serious charge of spousal abuse, Marcus finishing the academic term with the usual flurry of exams and papers and panicked students. Almost every evening Bob called Ruth, who continued to assure him she was fine.

They all got together at Alex and Carol's house in Los Angeles for a few days between Christmas and New Year's, as they usually did. Marcus noticed that Ruth looked older, or as if she hadn't been sleeping. Bob noticed it, too, and said something about it to his brother.

"I know," Alex said. "But she doesn't want to talk about it. Carol tried. If she was going to open up, it would be to Carol."

Bob nodded; he knew from a lifetime with her that Ruth would not want to burden either of her sons, adding to their own grief.

They exchanged gifts, sweaters and books mostly, and toys and puzzles for Lily. Ruth gave Jake's watch to Alex, his briefcase to Bob, and his wallet to her grandson Jay, as the three thanked her and smiled through their tears.

Carol and Bob cooked, and Alex, Ruth, and Marcus played endless games of Monopoly with Lily and Ruthie, Alex and Carol's daughter. Jay spent time with friends he had grown up with and, when he hung around the house, taught the girls how to play gin rummy and poker.

Bob and Alex had fought good naturedly over which of their daughters would get Ruth's name, but Ruthie was born before Lily's adoption from China was complete, and that was that.

"You know," Jake had said when Carol was first pregnant, "we're Jews. Technically, we're only supposed to name kids after dead people."

"We're not that Jewish," Ruth said. Everybody laughed, and Alex and Carol named their first-born Jacob, after Jake, and called him Jay for short.

"I think Lily has the makings of a card shark," Jay announced one afternoon. That didn't surprise Bob and Marcus at all; Lily was super-smart, and they were thinking of putting her in a school for gifted children. Her intelligence test scores were off the charts. The next day, the girls wanted to play cards again, but Jay, not wanting to lose, took them to see *Elf*—it played at a local movie palace dating to the 1940s, which the girls loved almost as much as the movie itself.

After dinner one night, Ruth asked Marcus to help her get

coffee and dessert.

"Marcus, in the kitchen?" Bob said good-naturedly. "What are you thinking?" Marcus was pretty much a disaster at cooking, which everyone knew, including Marcus.

Ruth laughed and Marcus got up and followed her. As she poured water into the coffeepot, her expression turned serious.

"I know this has been hard on him," Ruth said. "Of course it has. But I'm worried about his drinking."

Marcus felt a jolt. It was true, Bob had been drinking more since Jake died, but he didn't think anyone else had noticed. Bob never appeared drunk, but he was drinking sometimes during the day, something he had never done before. Marcus wasn't sure what was going on, if it was anything more than a short-term reaction to his father's death.

There was a long, awkward silence.

"You're right," Marcus said finally. "I'm a little worried about it too. He's about to turn forty, of course. That might be part of it." Marcus, ten years older than Bob, was almost fifty now, and he well remembered what turning forty was like.

"Forty is hard," Marcus went on. "Plus he's had hard cases at work. Law is a real grind. For Alex too. And I'm sure it was for Jake."

"Yes, it was. It's not an easy life," Ruth said.

What Marcus didn't say was that in addition to more drinking, Bob had been wanting more sex since Jake died. A lot more sex. Marcus could hardly keep up.

Ruth went on. "If it doesn't stop soon, talk to him about it. Or maybe talk to him now. When you're alone. Don't let it get out of control. Get him help if he needs it."

Marcus nodded, and Ruth patted him on the arm. He was touched that Ruth trusted him enough to talk about it, and impressed that she was sharp enough to have noticed, so soon after losing Jake.

And he knew she was right.

Marcus often thought about the ways in which Bob resembled both of his parents. He had Ruth's sense of fun and good cheer, most of the time, and he had Jake's logical brain and now, after years of practice, his father's equanimity about work. Alex was the opposite, in some ways; he had more of Jake's quiet, understated personality at home, less of his mother's. But he was anxious and excitable when it came to his work, which Marcus thought would have been Ruth's style if she had practiced law, as all three men did.

On their last evening in Los Angeles Marcus brought up Bob's birthday, a month away.

"Big bash, at our house. An extravaganza." Lily jumped up and clapped and sat in Marcus's lap.

Bob groaned. "Oh, God. Please, no. Turning forty is punishment enough."

"Oh, come on, it'll be fun," Ruth said, and Bob forced a smile. If it would make his mother happy, give her something to look forward to, he'd go along.

"Okay, okay. If you promise to make lots of poppy-seed cake," he said, smiling at Ruth, who threw her head back and laughed. Poppy-seed cake was her specialty, and Bob had loved it for as long as he could remember. They all talked about the date and where the LA folks could stay, since their house wouldn't hold everyone.

On the drive home the next day, Marcus needed to stop on campus, just off the freeway on their way back to central San Diego where they lived; a graduate student had promised to leave an overdue dissertation chapter in his mailbox. Bob and Lily stayed in the car; Marcus just needed to retrieve it.

The campus was deserted, not a soul anywhere; Marcus couldn't remember another time when absolutely no one was around. It felt weird. He took the elevator up to his floor and switched on the lights in the mailroom.

And there, on the floor, he saw the dead body of his senior colleague, Charles Silver.

3

Marcus froze and stared at the corpse. Chuck was well-dressed, as usual, in an expensive suit, silk tie, beautifully polished shoes, and Marcus saw no signs of violence or a struggle. He knew not to touch anything. As he stared at the body, he thought Silver looked smaller than the last time he'd seen him, as if he had lost weight.

After a few moments he snapped himself to attention. He went to his office, called campus security, then went out to the car and motioned for Bob to roll down his window. Lily was dozing in the back seat, so he whispered. He told Bob what had happened.

"Take Lily home, then come back. Becky can probably baby-sit."

Becky was a neighbor, sixteen, who often sat with Lily. Bob nodded.

"The police will want to talk to me, I have to be here. Come back and get me. Or wait at home for me to call. I don't know how long this will take."

"I'll come back. Just tell the police exactly what you saw, not a word more." Bob the lawyer was now talking.

Marcus nodded. Bob put his hand on top of Marcus's and then quickly got out and walked to the driver's side of the car.

Marcus watched the car drive away and suddenly felt very alone. He shivered. Several uniformed campus security cars were pulling up as he got close to the entrance to the building,

A campus officer vaguely recognized Marcus as a faculty member; opening the car's window, he said, "Sorry, Sir, the building is closed."

"I'm the one who called, officer. I found the body."

"In that case, please wait." The security men got out of their squad cars and said the San Diego police were on their way.

"Should I tell you what happened?" Marcus asked.

"No, Sir, let's wait for the police." Marcus nodded and put his hands in the pockets of his jacket and pulled up his collar; a cold wind was blowing in off the ocean. One of the officers rubbed his hands together against the wind.

Soon two police cars and a regulation-issue sedan pulled up, sirens blaring. Four uniformed officers and two plain-clothes detectives got out.

"Are you the one who found the body?" one of the detectives asked Marcus.

He nodded.

"Please come with us."

They rode the elevator up to the fourth floor. Marcus did his best to stay calm.

"Where is your office?" one detective asked.

"Down the hall, that way."

"All right, let's go there."

They walked down the darkened hallway, past the mailroom. The uniformed officers pulled yellow police tape out of their pockets and closed off the room. The body was in the same position as when Marcus found it.

Marcus turned on the lights in his office, sat behind his desk, and the two detectives took the two chairs in front of the desk. Marcus noticed that the office was cold; the heat must have been turned way down for the holiday break. He left his jacket on.

Both men took out notebooks and pens and introduced themselves, handing over business cards. One was named Mulroney, the other, Sanchez. Both looked to be around thirty-five or forty.

"Okay, tell us everything. Start with your name, your relation to the deceased, and how you came to be here on a quiet Saturday afternoon in the middle of Christmas vacation."

4

Marcus told the story as straightforwardly as he could: Driving down from LA, the graduate student's chapter, seeing the body.

"We'll need the name of that student and the names of people you were with in Los Angeles."

"Yes, of course." Marcus wrote it all down on a slip of paper, handed it to Sanchez. He vaguely remembered the student, Julie Klein, had said she was planning to go out of town as soon as she finished the chapter, although he didn't say as much; he wasn't sure he was remembering correctly.

"Was the chapter in your mailbox?"

Marcus realized that he had been so shocked by seeing the body that he didn't notice if the chapter was there. "I didn't even look," he said apologetically.

"How well did you know Professor Silver?"

Marcus remembered what Bob had said; tell them the truth, but as little as possible.

"Well, we've been colleagues for about ten years. We've been on committees together, socialized a bit, nothing out of the ordinary."

"So would you call him a personal friend?"

"No, not really. A colleague."

"Did he have a family?"

"Yes, he was married. To another faculty member, Emma Baker. She teaches French literature. And they have a young daughter."

"Did he have any enemies? Anyone who would want him dead?"

Marcus decided to tread carefully. "I can't think of anyone who would do this, no." He realized he hadn't answered the exact question he had been asked. In fact, there were a lot of people who disliked Chuck Silver, even hated him, both at UCSD and elsewhere. He was an intellectual bomb-thrower and loved a good fight. Loved it too much, Marcus often thought. And there were always rumors that Chuck had affairs, but Marcus never knew if the rumors were true or just typical academic gossip. Chuck was an academic high-flyer, and that meant people talked about him. Academic gossip could be vicious and not always accurate. It was one of the things Marcus disliked about his profession.

"What was his academic subject?"

"British history and literature, especially as it related to British imperialism." Marcus got up and retrieved a couple of Chuck's books from the bookshelves, put them in front of the detectives. "He was very well known. Not just in the U.S. but around the world."

The detectives looked at the books as if they were some kind of radioactive waste.

"You can't think of anyone who would want him dead?"

Marcus was starting to feel really anxious. "No. I cannot."

"Well," Mulroney said, as they both closed their notebooks and got up out of their chairs, "if you think of anything else that might help us, please call. Anything at all, sometimes the smallest detail can be important."

Marcus knew that was true from talking to Bob about some of his cases. He nodded.

"Do you have a business card?"

Marcus opened a desk drawer and handed one over.

"Please write your home address and phone number on the back."

Marcus did as he was told, handed it over, and the officers left, after telling him not to go out of town without notifying them. He wondered if he was now a suspect. Bob, who had defended his share of murderers, had once said you never want to be the person who finds the body; it makes you suspicious from the get-go.

He let out a deep breath. He stared out the window, which provided a glimpse of the ocean. He felt completely exhausted. Then he realized he should wait for Bob in front of the building, since they probably wouldn't let anyone else inside.

As he walked past the mailroom, he saw that a swarm of new police personnel had arrived; they were dusting for fingerprints and someone was examining the body, which had been turned over. Extra lights had been set up and cameras clicked. Mulroney and Sanchez stood to the side, watching. Marcus saw that the dissertation chapter was in his mail slot, but he realized they wouldn't let him retrieve it.

He took the elevator down and waited outside for Bob. Still more campus security officers were milling around, and they had put up traffic barriers to keep people away from the entrance, although there was no one around anywhere.

"Well, that was fun," he said when Bob pulled up and he got into the car.

5

The murder led the local TV news that evening and hit the front page of the local newspaper Sunday morning. Police were quoted as saying there was "strong evidence" of "foul play" and that the condition of the body suggested Silver had been dead for fifteen to twenty hours when he was discovered.

UCSD was a major institution in San Diego, more woven into the fabric of local life than the sister campuses in Los Angeles or Berkeley in the Bay Area. The local news covered the school extensively. Many thought the founding of the campus in 1960 was the true beginning of San Diego's history as a major city. It was a major player in the city's biotech boom.

Everyone was in a somber mood at dinner that night, even Lily, who could tell something was wrong even though they didn't say anything about the murder. They all went to bed early.

The phone kept ringing all morning Sunday, colleagues, university officials; everyone wanted to hear the story. For a while Marcus took it off the hook. The news hadn't mentioned Marcus by name but somehow word had gotten out that he found the body. Word always gets out in academia, he knew. It often drove him crazy.

Maggie Garner, the Senior Vice Chancellor—the chief academic officer of the sprawling campus—called around noon and told Marcus, to his surprise, that Silver's wife Emma wanted to see him that evening, and that she suggested bringing Bob.

"She's met Bob, she knows he's a lawyer, and she may want some legal advice at this point," Maggie said.

Marcus could think of almost nothing he'd want to do less than see Emma that evening, but he knew he couldn't say no. They arranged to meet at the Silvers' La Jolla home at 8:30, and, when he got off the phone, he told Bob, who groaned.

"Oh God. Do I have to?"

"You don't have to take her as a client. She may just need advice. How to act during a murder investigation. What to say to the police. The estate. Who knows. It could be painless."

Marcus knew that probably wasn't true, but didn't know what else to say.

"Why don't you give Lily lunch and then take a rest. I'll do a grocery run."

Bob nodded.

Marcus went to the Ralph's in Hillcrest. It wasn't the closest grocery store to their house in Normal Heights but it was the best, a kind of social hub for gay community where lots of their friends shopped. It was always busy.

Sure enough, Marcus ran into several people there, including some friends and another UCSD colleague, Rudd Martin, who naturally wanted to hear about Chuck. Marcus told him a brief version of the story as they both leaned over their shopping carts in the frozen food aisle.

Rudd, short for Rudolph, was pensive. He was well-dressed, as usual, including a long, colorful scarf tied around his neck, and he looked, as always, like a male model who belonged in an ad for high fashion. Like Emma Baker, he studied French literature.

"Did it look like a murder?" Rudd asked, a little too excitedly, Marcus thought.

"I don't know," Marcus answered truthfully. "All I saw was the body, just for a moment. I didn't see any blood or anything like that."

"Poor Emma, poor Chloe," Rudd responded. Chloe was Emma and Chuck's daughter. Marcus tried to remember how old she was. "Of course," Rudd added, "money won't be a problem, I'm sure. They'll be fine."

For a moment Rudd seemed lost in thought. They all had interacted on campus, Rudd, Emma, Chuck, Marcus; all of them studied literature or rhetoric one way or another and had done some typical socializing. They had all served on dissertation committees together.

"I wonder," Rudd said, "if it could have been someone from the MLA."

Marcus hadn't thought of that and was startled. The MLA, the Modern Language Association, had just held its annual meeting in San Diego. Marcus had been slated to appear on a panel but canceled when Jake died, and he had completely forgotten about the conference.

The MLA was a huge annual convention of scholars studying literature of all kinds. It usually convened between Christmas and New Year's, and that meant hundreds, if not thousands, of scholars who knew Chuck or his work had been in town. Marcus didn't know for sure, but he imagined both Emma and Chuck had attended. Although the official conference didn't begin until the 27th that year, if Marcus was remembering correctly, the event had grown so unwieldy and huge that some people arrived early, and various unofficial groupings of scholars held small sessions or meetings before the official opening, especially if the setting was a pleasant or warm place to be, as San Diego was. And some people, especially younger scholars, just showed up early to spend the holiday with friends and see the local sites.

All this, he realized, would make the job of finding the killer extremely tricky.

"I mean, Charles got into a shouting match at a panel about Arabic literature," Rudd added.

"That doesn't surprise me," Marcus said. "Chuck had strong feelings there."

Chuck had seen the war raging in Iraq as a disaster, Marcus knew, and was a fierce critic of what he called the Cheney-Rumsfeld administration. He had gone so far as to publicly label Cheney a war criminal. He saw President Bush as the hapless puppet of the American war machine; he called him "W," as did many of his critics, because of his middle name, Walker. Pretty much everyone at UCSD hated Bush and loved Al Gore, who had been mentored on environmental issues by Roger Revelle, one of the

founders of UCSD; the campus had become an early hotbed of
environmentalism. One of the undergraduate colleges was named
in Revelle's honor. The 2000 election and Gore's loss by a few
hundred votes in Florida still rankled almost everyone they knew.

The Iraq war, Chuck thought, was a remnant of the way great
empires had always carved up the world, the Spanish, the British, the
French, and, lately, what he liked to call the American Imperium.
In fact, the heart of Chuck's work had been tracing the cultural
and literary impact of British imperialism. He was one of the best
scholars to explore in depth the cruelty of the British in India, in
South Africa, and elsewhere. That, and his anti-Zionism, despite
being Jewish himself, made him both famous and notorious, and
his willingness to talk about contemporary politics had made him
a darling of the Left and a popular source for journalists. He had
even been interviewed on television by Charlie Rose. His name
appeared in the press at least a few times every year. He never shied
away from an argument or a fight. Or publicity.

"Well," Marcus said finally, "I've got to get this stuff into the
fridge."

"Of course," Rudd said. "A bientôt."

Marcus thought about the MLA on the drive home.

"Quel mess," he mumbled to himself.

6

Bob and Lily were both napping. Zelda was asleep on Lily's
bed and thumped her tail once when Marcus peered into
the room. They had tried to keep the dog off the beds but it was
hopeless. When they would tell her to get down she would comply,
but when she gave them a hopeless, sad look and let out a little
cry, they relented. She and Lily were inseparable, as Lily had been

with Oscar, their previous Golden, who had died of old age at 14. Putting him down was one of the worst experiences Marcus could remember. Lily cried for weeks. For the first few days after he died Marcus kept going to the patio door to let him back in the house, but of course he wasn't in the yard.

Marcus put the groceries away and then retrieved the MLA program from his study. Chuck had been on two panels, Emma on one. On Chuck's he saw other names he recognized as intellectual foes of Chuck's, and he was sure there had been fireworks.

He went into the bedroom, kicked off his shoes, and settled down on his side of the bed. Bob stirred and put his head on his shoulder. They slept for a long time, then woke when they heard Lily and Zelda in the living room.

Bob made dinner, a vegetable lasagna, and they arranged for Cathy to sit with Lily while they would be out.

"I'm getting big, you know," Lily said. "Maybe I don't need a baby sitter." She was 11.

"Eleven going on twenty," Bob said.

They both smiled, and both felt a pang; she was growing up fast.

"You like Cathy, don't you?" Marcus asked.

"Yeah, she's great."

"Another year or so," Bob said, "and then we'll let you stay home alone. If you promise not to set the house on fire of throw any crazy parties."

Lily giggled. Hearing her laugh was one of their greatest pleasures.

All three of them loved their house. It was a typical but spacious California bungalow from the 1920s, stucco, with a fireplace and wood floors and three original bedrooms. They had put an addition on the back of the house, a bedroom, bath, and playroom for Lily, as well as a large deck and patio. The construction was a pain in the neck and took forever, but in the end they were happy with the result.

After dinner they showered and dressed for the meeting with Emma, which they dreaded. It was still quite chilly, especially at night, and both wore sweaters and top coats.

They drove up to La Jolla, saying little.

7

The house was near campus, a block from the ocean. It was a grand place, a large midcentury ranch that they had renovated and expanded, with a huge patio and a pool; bob and Marcus had been there a few times for receptions or parties. As arranged, they met Vice Chancellor Garner on the street. She'd arrived first and was leaning against her car. She was dressed as she dressed for work, in an elegant wool suit with the collar pulled up, high heels, and leather gloves. She seemed to be scowling—probably because she was cold, Marcus thought—but softened her expression as they drove up. After quick greetings, Maggie got back into her car and they both pulled into the long driveway. Maggie rang the front doorbell. While they waited, they could hear the ocean, a block away. There was a heavy, cold mist in the air.

A man none of them recognized opened the door, a distinguished looking, elegantly dressed middle-aged man who introduced himself as Eugene, Emma's brother. He ushered them into the large living room where Emma was waiting. A fire burned in the large stone fireplace. The lights were dimmed. It was a spacious room furnished carefully with antiques coupled with tasteful modern furniture. Marcus remembered how comfortable the sofas were; they were filled with down.

Emma greeted Maggie, who gave her a slight, somewhat stiff

hug, then shook Marcus's hand and Bob's. Eugene offered them drinks, which they declined. Everyone sat. Both Eugene and Emma were sipping what smelled like brandy.

Maggie spoke first.

"Emma, you know how sorry we all are, how horrible it is for this to have happened."

Emma gave a slight smile and nod and took another sip of her brandy. She was dressed in black, a long-sleeved sweater, slacks, low heels. No jewelry except her gold wedding ring, which she stared at for a moment. Her chestnut hair tumbled to her shoulders; on campus, she usually wore it up. She had clearly been crying.

"How is Chloe?" Maggie asked.

"She's managing remarkably well. I'm not sure she really understands yet."

Everyone nodded slightly.

"Are you sure none of you want some brandy?" Emma asked. "It's very good. Eugene brought it over from London."

"Actually," Bob said, "I'm not driving. I'd try some."

Eugene got up to fetch another glass.

"So, you're all wondering why I asked you here. It's simple, really. I'm at sea. The police have been here once, asking what you'd expect them to ask, and they say they'll be back. I don't know what to say to them."

She turned toward Bob.

"And I wonder if they suspect me in some way. If I should have a lawyer here when they talk to me next time. Or if I should speak to them at all." She sipped her brandy, then went on.

"Bob, I know you have experience with . . . this sort of thing. I hope you don't mind my asking. I didn't know who else to ask."

"No, I don't mind at all," which of course wasn't true, Marcus knew. Then, slightly more businesslike, he continued. "Let's start with the first police interview. Did it sound like they were suspicious?"

Emma thought for a moment. "I'm not sure. Not really. I have so little experience with them. I've never talked to the police about anything, really, in my life."

"What did they ask?"

"Well, they think the murder took place sometime on Friday, probably in the afternoon or evening. He was shot. With a small revolver. In the back."

Her voice sounded slightly shaky, not at all in command as she was in the classroom. She and Bob each took another sip of brandy, and she continued. Marcus shuddered when he heard Chuck had been shot in the back.

"They wanted to know my whereabouts on Friday. I was at the conference almost all day. With lots of people around. I gave them the names of people who could vouch for that. I was here in the morning, and our maid was here, and Chloe. I called the maid into the room to confirm that. Then I was at the conference."

"Well, then I imagine you're not a suspect."

He smiled reassuringly. What he didn't say was that the police might suspect that Emma hired someone to kill her husband. They always speculate about such things when the people involved are well off, he knew. Marcus was thinking the same thing, and he wondered, for the first time, about the state of Chuck and Emma's marriage.

Emma and Eugene both looked relieved after hearing Bob's reply. So did Maggie Garner.

"What else did they ask?"

"They asked if Charles had enemies." Emma always called Chuck "Charles," for some reason. Everyone else called him "Chuck."

"And what did you say?"

"Well, I got very flustered. I didn't know what kind of 'enemy' they meant. I mean, there were scores of people he tangled with over intellectual matters, political matters. You know that, Marcus."

"Indeed."

"But does that make any of them murder suspects? I didn't know what to say."

"How did you answer?" Bob asked.

"I said I couldn't think of anyone who would do this, even though Charles took some controversial positions."

"That was the right thing to say."

Again, Emma looked relieved. She took a long sip of brandy and paused for a moment.

"There's something else I could use your help with. I'd like to hire a private investigator. I want to find out who did this."

And then she added something both Marcus and Bob thought was quite odd.

"For Chloe. I thought you could recommend someone."

Marcus spoke up, looking at Bob. "Jason?"

Emma looked expectantly at Bob. "Who is that?"

"Jason Thompson. He worked as my investigator for many years. Before that, he was a police detective. He's now independent. A good friend."

Eugene spoke. "Does he know what he's doing?"

"Yes, absolutely," Bob said. "He's very good at his job. I can talk to him, find out if he's available."

Emma looked hopeful. "That would be marvelous. If you feel comfortable."

"I do. But there's something to think about. The police, I'm sure, will do what they can." Bob didn't really believe that; he had seen too many sloppy police investigations. But he didn't want to complicate things or make Emma even more nervous.

"They don't always take kindly to a private investigator shadowing them, especially on a high-profile case, which this is. You might want to wait, see if the official investigation gets anywhere."

"No," Emma said firmly. "I want my own investigation here. From the beginning. Whatever it costs."

Bob pursed his lips. "Okay. I'll talk to Jason first thing in the morning."

Emma stood, and so did everyone else. "Thank you." And at that, she did something everyone found rather odd; she walked over and kissed Bob on the cheek.

Bob noticed her expensive perfume.

"Please excuse me for kicking you out so quickly, I'm just exhausted."

"Of course," Maggie said. "No need to apologize. Call me if you need anything. Anything at all. Have you had a chance to think about the funeral?"

"No funeral. Charles made his wishes about that clear. We might have a memorial service in a few weeks."

Maggie nodded, and they all walked to the front door, which Eugene held open.

"By the way, you're right," Bob said. "That brandy was amazing."

8

On the way home, Marcus asked Bob if he thought Jason would take the case.

"I don't know. I think it will depend on whether he's free. And whether he thinks he can help. With that convention here, there could be so many suspects, right? He might not want to get into it. This doesn't really sound like his kind of case."

Marcus nodded.

"Emma is much younger than Chuck, isn't she?" Bob said after a moment.

Marcus had never really thought about that. "Yes, actually, now that you mention it."

"Is it his first marriage?"

"No, second. His first wife died just before he came to UCSD. I think that's one of the reasons he left Columbia, for a fresh start."

"How did she die, the first wife?"

"Cancer. Apparently after a long struggle."

"And Chuck was a controversial figure?"

"Yes. Highly controversial. Famous for it. He took a lot of positions about contemporary politics. Very trendy, very left. The press seemed to loved him."

"Was he a serious scholar?"

"Definitely. At least five books. Maybe more. All well received. In demand as a speaker. Although . . ."

"Although?"

"Maybe a little less in demand lately."

They were quiet for a while. Finally, Bob asked the question he had wanted to ask all day.

"Do you think Emma could have wanted him dead?"

Marcus was taken aback. "I don't think so, but I really didn't know them that well. I suppose it's possible. You never know about a marriage, do you?"

"No," Bob admitted. "You don't. I mean, think of the Clintons. Everyone assumed it was an arrangement, a façade. She could have divorced him after they left the White House and she went to the Senate, but she didn't."

"True," Marcus said. "But it seems like they live separate lives. He's with his house in Westchester, she with hers in D.C."

"Jason would have to get into the nitty-gritty of the marriage,"

Bob said. "I mean, you always suspect the spouse. If I ever get shot, you'll need a good lawyer."

Marcus laughed.

"It's actually smart of Emma to have spoken to us," Bob added. "And to want an investigation. But . . ."

"But?"

"If she needs a lawyer, for real, I wouldn't be able to take the case. We've been to their house as guests a few of times. You work with her. You knew Chuck. Too close. Conflict of interest."

"Right. But you could find her someone?"

"Yes, of course. Do you think . . ." Bob hesitated.

"What?"

"Do you think either of them played around?"

Marcus had wondered that himself. "I don't know. I suppose it's possible."

"But you never picked up a whiff of marital trouble?"

"No, not really. I mean, Emma is quite beautiful. Chuck was famous. They both knew a lot of people, moved in chic circles. And . . ."

"And?"

"I don't know. I try not to pay attention to gossip. But La Jolla. You hear rumors."

"Of?"

"Of some people living life in the fast lane. You know, sex, drugs, jet-setting."

"And you said Chuck traveled a lot."

"Yes, he was always jetting off. In fact at one point he got into hot water for canceling too many classes."

Bob seemed lost in thought.

When they got home, they thanked Cathy for baby-sitting and gave her their Christmas present, a sweater that matched her green eyes. She hugged them both with real enthusiasm. Lily was in her pajamas, ready for bed. While Marcus took her in to say good-night, Bob called Jason.

He gave the detective a quick outline of the case, and Jason said to come to his place first thing in the morning, and to bring Marcus.

Bob and Marcus built a fire and listened to some old jazz records, with Zelda at their feet. Bob laid his head in Marcus's lap on the couch.

"Come on, old man, let's go to bed," Bob said after a while, pulling Marcus up from the couch. "I'm going to ravish you."

9

In the morning Zelda woke them up early, as usual, and, after letting her into the yard and feeding her, Bob made pancakes. Lily had a play date with a school friend and they dropped her off on their way to Jason's.

"Be good," Bob said.

"I'm always good," Lily said. "With other people."

"Wow," Marcus said as they watched her walk up to the house. "Sass. She's growing up."

"Yeah. Soon she'll be a teenager."

"Well, that will be an experience."

They drove off.

Jason had just bought his first house in Talmadge, an up-and-coming neighborhood east of Normal Heights, where Bob and Marcus lived. His private practice seemed to be thriving.

When they rang the doorbell, a young man with a perfect body and a marine haircut opened the door. He was dressed in a towel. Jason had a never-ending stream of younger boyfriends, most from the military. "So many marines, so little time," he liked to say.

"Hi, I'm Zach. Jason's in the kitchen." His smile was dazzling.

"He belongs in *Top Gun*," Bob whispered.

Jason was standing at the stove, dressed casually and with bare feet, making scrambled eggs.

"Hey. Have you guys eaten? There's coffee."

Bob poured them both cups while Jason finished the eggs. Zach reappeared, dressed in jeans and a white T-shirt, carrying a leather jacket, and announced he had to get going. He kissed Jason and grabbed a piece of toast.

"So how long has this one been around?" Bob asked with a smile after Zach left.

"Mmm, I'd have to check the roster. A few weeks."

"And you recite poetry to each other and talk of the soul, right?" Marcus teased.

Jason laughed. "If this one has a soul, it's buried somewhere deep in that granite chest."

"It's amazing," Bob said, "what a marine can do for a simple white T-shirt." He sighed.

They settled around the breakfast table, a little nook. Sun was streaming in through the windows. The temperature finally seemed to be moderating after a long cold snap.

"So. Tell me about this murder."

They told the story. Jason listened carefully as he ate, then said what Bob expected him to say.

"The cops won't like it, a private eye at this point. It might even suggest to them that she's guilty."

"Right," Bob said. "I told her she might want to wait, see how the investigation goes. But she seemed determined. You could tell her the same thing, see if she's willing to wait. She might be, if she hears it from you."

"Do you suspect her?"

"Not sure either way," Bob said. "Marcus knows them better."

"As colleagues," Marcus said quickly. "Not really as friends. I just don't know. I mean, they seemed happy enough, but I didn't spend a lot of time with either one of them."

"I don't know," Jason said after a moment. "I mean, I don't know anything about their world. Your world," he said, looking at Marcus. "It sounds like he was a kind of celebrity, and had enemies. There could be a long list of suspects. Messy case."

"Would you at least talk to her? Get a feel for things?" Marcus asked.

Jason thought for a moment. "Okay, but you'll need to be there with me. Make the introduction, listen, tell me if I'm missing anything, or if anything seems off."

Marcus nodded.

"I'm free this afternoon, if she is. Otherwise, it'll have to wait until after New Year's. I promised to take Zach to Big Bear. He's from Minnesota, he misses the snow. Not that we spend a lot of time on the slopes," Jason added.

Bob smirked.

"I'll call her now," he said. He pulled a slip of paper from his pocket and dialed the kitchen phone.

He quickly arranged a meeting for that afternoon at 4:00, hung up, and turned to Jason. "I'll pick you up at 3:30."

Jason nodded. "In the meantime, make a list of Silver's academic enemies. See what you can find out what happened at that conference . . . what's it called? The MBA?"

Marcus laughed. "The MLA. The Modern Language Association."

"Right. You weren't there?"

"No. I was supposed to be, but then Jake died. I can ask around." Marcus thought about his conversation with Rudd in the grocery store.

Bob dropped Marcus at home and then went to his office to

do some paperwork. At home Marcus settled in his study to work on his latest article, what he hoped would be a new interpretation of Thoreau and his relationship with the other Transcendentalists, and, if it panned out, the beginning of a new book. But Zelda came in with her "if you don't take me for a walk right now I'll report you to the authorities" look, so he took her for a jaunt around the neighborhood, where she wagged her tail and greeted everyone they met. She wanted to go into Cathy's house, a few doors down from theirs, but Marcus pulled her away.

Back home, Marcus forgot about his article and tried to come up with a list of Chuck Silver's enemies. At first he drew a blank, but then he came up with a few names.

There was Ed Peterson, in UCSD's English department, who was a fierce intellectual critic of Chuck's. They had had shouting matches at meetings.

Sandra Bernstein at Berkeley, a staunch defender of Israel. She and Chuck had had several nasty disputes in prominent public venues like *The New York Review of Books*.

And Liam Frasier at the University of Chicago, who had written scathing reviews of two of Chuck's books, reviews that many people, even some of Chuck's critics, thought were over the top.

But these were intellectual foes, Marcus realized, not personal ones. He got up and started to pace around his study.

It just didn't feel possible that their disagreements with Chuck, however fierce, could lead to murder, could lead to someone shooting Chuck with a revolver, murdering him in cold blood in a mailroom on a deserted campus right after Christmas.

He resumed pacing.

Or maybe he just didn't want to believe that could happen in the hallowed halls academe. Despite everything, despite his own doubts and troubles along the way, Marcus still thought of university life as a noble calling.

Professors didn't do such things, unless they were insane.

Marcus was wrestling with that thought when he remembered he should contact Rudd Martin, find out more about what had happened at the MLA.

Rudd picked up on the first ring and suggested they meet for lunch.

10

They met at La Vache, a new, vaguely French restaurant in a strip mall near the center of Hillcrest. After the usual small talk, Marcus asked him for an account of what had happened at the MLA.

"Well, it was quite the scene," Rudd said dramatically, sipping his white wine. Most of what Rudd said was dramatic. Marcus thought that dramatic speech was an occupational hazard for professors, in fact, a result of constantly needing to make ideas and texts interesting to bored undergraduates. It was something he tried to guard against outside the classroom, although more than once Bob had told him to switch off lecture mode.

"It was a packed session, at least 200 people in a big ballroom," Rudd went on. "Maybe more. A roundtable on contemporary Arabic lit. Charles did his usual thing, defending Palestinians, blaming other Arabic states for not supporting the cause strongly enough, criticizing Israel, criticizing American support for Israel, 'billions for butchery' he said. The literature of the oppressed. You know the drill."

"I do. And?"

"And Simon Templeton was there."

"Oh." Templeton was probably Silver's most consistent and

angry critic, from the UK, although at the moment Marcus couldn't remember if he was at Oxford or Cambridge.

"Yes. He's visiting at UCLA this year."

"Ah. I didn't know."

"Simon stood up and really laid into Charles. I mean, both barrels blazing. Name calling. Insults. They were both enraged. It was quite the scene. People in the audience literally gasped."

"I see. I'm sorry I missed it. Was Emma there?"

"Yes, she was in the audience. She didn't say anything. She looked uncomfortable."

"Not surprising. What happened after the panel?"

"Well, I'm not exactly sure. Charles and Templeton did leave the room together. They both looked furious. Emma disappeared."

Those might be important details, Marcus realized.

"What time was the panel?"

"The 1:30 slot. It was all anyone could talk for the rest of afternoon. In the hallways, at the hotel bars."

"I see. Do you know Templeton?"

"I've met him a few times. Don't know him all that well. I do know . . ."

"Yes?"

"Well, it's rumor, but the word is he and Emma were at one time involved," Rudd said.

Marcus sat back. "Was that before or after she and Chuck were married?"

Rudd thought for a moment. "I'm not sure. Before, I imagine."

"Well, thanks for filling me in." At the mention of Emma, Marcus suddenly felt uncomfortable, although he wasn't sure why. He steered the conversation to small talk.

After they said good-bye out on the sidewalk, Marcus realized Rudd had called Silver "Charles." And then he remembered that the previous year, when she was on leave, Emma had spent a considerable amount of time in London, doing research at the British Museum.

And, Marcus realized, if Templeton had driven back to UCLA after that panel, he would have driven right past the UCSD campus. Right around the time the police were saying Chuck had been shot.

He let out a deep breath.

11

It was 2:30. Marcus drove home and found Bob working at the dining room table with Anna, his law partner. She got up and, effusive as ever, hugged Marcus tightly and wished him a happy new year. Marcus sat with them for a few minutes and then changed clothes and left to pick up Jason for their meeting with Emma.

"I'll make dinner," Bob said. "Bring Jason if he wants to come. We'll still be working," he added, pointing to the pile of the documents spread out on the table in front of them.

Marcus noticed Bob had a glass of wine in front of him.

"Don't work too hard," he said, as he gathered up his keys and a light jacket.

Jason was waiting in front of his house, and there was little traffic as they made their way up to La Jolla.

"Tell me what you can about this couple," Jason said.

"Well," Marcus said, "in academia, they're a power couple. He's extremely well-known, she less so. It's a second marriage for him, first for her. They have a young daughter. They both are well plugged in to a network of international scholars, which is not surprising, given their fields."

"Remind me . . ."

"British lit and politics for him, French for her."

"Right."

"I'm not sure how long they've been together. Maybe ten years."

"Wealth?"

"Yes. He's from a prominent family in San Francisco. She's from a more modest background in the Midwest, I forget exactly where. Maybe St. Louis. She won a scholarship to Vassar, then went on to a fellowship at Yale for her PhD."

"So she married up?"

Marcus had never thought of it that way. "Yes, you could say that."

"And you never picked up any sense of trouble between them?"

"No, but I really didn't know them well. We've been on some committees together on campus, I've been to a few social events at their house, big events, lots of people around. But that's about it."

"How would you describe their personalities?"

Marcus thought for a moment. "He was combative, loved nothing more than a good argument. Or fight. She's quite reserved. Her style is almost . . ."

"Almost?"

"Almost old world. Certainly old fashioned. A proper lady."

"So, a case of opposites attracting?"

"Yes, possibly." Bob had always said Jason was perceptive about people, and his judgments were almost always on the money.

"And his combativeness, did it ever get out of hand?"

Marcus wanted to answer carefully. "It depends who you ask."

Jason smirked. "You should have been a politician."

"God, never. I'd rather dig ditches."

"Oh, yeah. I can just see you in the working class. You'd last two days. What happened at this conference that just ended?"

Marcus recounted what he had heard from Rudd, then said, "But . . ."

"But?" Jason asked.

"Rudd, who told me the story, has a tendency to dramatize. So . . ."

"Take what he says with a grain of salt?"

"Yes, I would. Maybe a whole salt-shaker's worth. We can ask Emma about it, she was apparently in the audience."

They pulled into the driveway, and Emma opened the front door just as they reached it. She flashed a smile at Jason and led them into the living room. A maid approached with a tray carrying expensive-looking china and silver. Emma offered tea, which they both accepted. Marcus noticed that the maid had brought both lemon and cream, as they did in upscale European hotels.

"So," Emma said, looking straight at Jason, in a manner Marcus thought slightly seductive, "can you find out who did this to my husband?"

"I can try, certainly, but it might not be the wisest thing to do right now."

"Why is that?"

"Well, for one thing, a spouse is an automatic suspect in a situation like this. If the police see that you've hired a private investigator, it's a natural assumption for them that you're hiding something."

"I'm willing to take that chance," Emma replied, tossing her hair away from her face. There was something about her demeanor that unsettled Marcus; this was not the same woman he had seen just the night before. She was wearing a revealing charcoal-colored blouse over dark charcoal slacks, high heels, bracelets on her arms. Makeup.

"And," Jason went on, "this could be an expensive undertaking. As Marcus has explained to me, a major conference just ended, and people are returning to wherever they came from, all over the country. Some of them may have to be interviewed. That could involve travel expenses."

"I understand. Whatever it costs."

"All right. Marcus has told me about an incident during a panel at this conference on Friday. I understand you were there. Can you tell me what happened?"

Emma got up and went to a bar and poured herself a sherry. She offered some to Marcus and Jason; both declined. She sat back down and narrated the story, which closely matched what Rudd had told Marcus.

"Do you think this professor, Templeton, could have wanted your husband dead?"

She paused. "Yes. You see . . ."

"Yes?"

"Simon and I were involved once. So there were personal factors as well as professional."

"When were you involved?"

"Before I met Charles, about a dozen years ago, when I was doing research for my doctorate in London and Paris. He's based at Oxford."

"And the affair ended when you married Professor Silver?"

Emma took a sip of her sherry.

"Yes. We still saw each other from time to time, as friends, colleagues. Though not recently. Not for several years."

"I see." Jason took a sip of his tea, then went on. "Forgive me for asking this, but did you ever suspect your husband of having an affair?"

Emma paused again. She looked out the window at the patio and pool. "Yes. Charles had affairs." She was completely calm.

Jason waited for her to say more.

"I gave my husband the space he needed," she said simply, and turned back to look at Jason.

"I see."

"Perhaps that sounds strange. But it worked for us."

"And you're sure your affair with Mr. Templeton ended when you married Mr. Silver?"

"Of course I'm sure," she said with a little laugh.

"Did you see Templeton this week, at that conference?"

"Yes. We had lunch." She smiled. "Just lunch."

"What day was that?"

"Thursday. We went to the Budapest Café. I imagine Simon has an American Express receipt."

"And?"

"And, to my surprise, he wanted us to get back together. He's just been divorced."

"And?"

"I told him I wasn't interested."

"I see. Thank you for your candor." Jason took a gulp of tea. "Was your husband involved with anyone just recently?"

"I don't know for certain. I never wanted to know the details. It was one of our . . ."

"Rules?" Jason offered.

"Practices."

Jason waited.

"Charles has been quite busy with a new book." Then Emma looked over at Marcus for the first time. "Poor Marcus, I'm shocking you, aren't I?"

Marcus wondered what his face was showing. He tried to smile. "A little, to be honest."

She smiled, got up, poured herself more sherry.

"Charles did not consider monogamy to be a natural state," she said, sitting again. "And I'm not sure men are capable of it, over the long haul, without becoming miserable. But we did love each other. We both loved our life with Chloe. I'd say the fact that

I gave Charles his freedom made the marriage stronger."

Jason was scribbling notes.

Emma got up. "Please excuse me for a moment. I need to check on my daughter."

12

After she left the room, Jason and Marcus looked at each other. Jason gave a little shrug; Marcus knew he probably agreed with Emma about monogamy for men.

Marcus let out a deep breath and wondered why he himself was different. He never even thought about sex with anyone but Bob since they first met. He recognized attractiveness in men, admired it, but that was all. He wondered if that made him provincial, conventional.

When Emma returned to the room, she was carrying pieces of paper.

"I made some lists last night." She handed them to Jason. "The first is a list of Charles's foes, people I could imagine wanting him . . . out of the picture. The second is a list of women I know or suspect Charles has been involved with. But I'm not certain. About any of them."

"Thank you, this will be very helpful."

"And you'll want to check out the apartment, I imagine."

"Apartment?" Jason snapped to full attention.

"Yes, Charles kept a small apartment, down near Tourmaline."

Tourmaline was a beach in North San Diego, just south of the La Jolla town line, famous with surfers. It was a lovely spot hidden away behind a cliff, in a neighborhood called Pacific Beach.

"He worked there sometimes. Charles needed absolute quiet when he was writing. And with our young daughter, and a maid, he needed a hideaway. I never used it. In fact, I've never been there. But here's the address." She handed Jason another slip of paper. "The building caretaker can let you in. He lives there. His name is Jenkins. I'll give him your name."

"Is there anyone beside this Professor Templeton that you, well, uh . . . suspect? Any recent incidents?"

"I've put an asterisk next to two names on that list. I can tell you more about them, but right now, you'll have to excuse me. I promised Chloe we'd spend some time together. She's quite upset, as I'm sure you can imagine."

Jason said they would need to meet again, sign a contract, discuss his fee, and so forth, but that all that could wait until Monday morning. They arranged to meet at 10 a.m.

"Have the police contacted you again?" Jason asked as everyone got up.

"They'll be here tomorrow."

"One piece of advice. Answer their questions honestly, but don't reveal too much about your marriage, if you can avoid it. Don't withhold information, but don't volunteer it, either. No lists."

"All right, if you say so."

"And thank you again for being so candid."

Emma ushered them to the front door and thanked them for coming. She put her hand on Jason's arm as he walked out and, Marcus thought, left it there a little too long.

When they got into the car, they looked at each other.

"Now that," Jason said, "Is one cool customer. She reminds me of Audrey Hepburn in that crime caper. The one where she was married to a Frenchman but didn't know anything about him. The husband gets knocked off at the beginning of the movie."

"Oh, yes. *Charade.*" Marcus chuckled to himself, remembering the first time he'd seen the film with Bob.

"Of course," Jason said as they got on the road, "a wife in

this situation could supply names of suspects to deflect attention from herself."

"Yes, I thought of that," Marcus replied. He was thinking hard. "Why did you tell her not to give the lists to the police?"

"Because they will inevitably think the lists are a deflection, even more than I suspect it. I've seen it too many times."

"Could she have done it?" Marcus asked.

"I suppose. But then why would she hire a private eye? She wouldn't be so anxious to find the murderer. She'd just let the police fumble around, hoping they wouldn't find anything."

"Maybe hiring you is also a deflection."

"Yes, that's possible. Always suspect the spouse, or the boyfriend or girlfriend. Rule number one."

"I don't know how you guys do it, deal with this sort of thing all the time. It would drive me nuts."

"You get used to it. Mostly."

They rode in silence for a while.

"Bob is cooking dinner. You're invited."

"Thanks, wish I could, but I've got plans."

"The cute marine?"

Jason smiled. "Yeah, Zach. I'm kinda hoping. . ."

Marcus looked at him.

"I'm kinda hoping he might be a keeper."

Marcus was surprised; he and Bob didn't think Jason would ever settle down. But he had bought a house and was approaching mid-life. Everyone thought Jason was gorgeous and that he looked like the 1950s closeted heartthrob Tab Hunter, and could have anyone he wanted, which seemed to have been true. But these days, he looked more like the older Tab Hunter, although that hadn't seem to slow him down, romance-wise. He was still a hunk.

"Take a look at those lists, tell me if you recognize any names."

Three names were familiar to Marcus—Fred Isaacson and Ed

Peterson, both UCSD professors, and Julie Klein, the graduate student with the late dissertation chapter that had sent Marcus to the mailroom that day. Both Peterson and Klein had asterisks next to their names. Marcus told Jason about all of them.

"Isaacson is an historian, and there are plans to set up a Center on campus for the study of the Middle East. Isaacson and Silver have very different ideas about how it should be organized. My guess is, they both wanted to be named director. At least that's the talk around campus. Julie Klein is a graduate student, writing her dissertation. Both Silver and I were on her committee. Peterson and Silver have clashed over various issues on campus over the years."

"Interesting. Could Julie Klein have been having an affair with Silver?"

Marcus didn't want to believe it, but answered truthfully. "It's certainly possible. That kind of thing does still go on, even though it's against the rules. And dangerous, for the faculty member."

Jason seemed to be thinking hard. "Who would I talk to on campus to get an overview on all this?"

"Maggie Garner. She's the SVC."

"SVC?"

"Senior Vice Chancellor. Chief academic officer. Like a Provost. The boss."

"The Chancellor isn't the boss?"

"Not for day-to-day academic matters. He mostly deals with the big picture, donors, that type of thing."

"Will this SVC talk to me?"

"Yes, I think so. She'll want this crime solved and out of the news as soon as possible."

"And what can you tell me about this Templeton?"

"Not much. I don't know him personally. Well-known scholar. As well-known in the UK as Silver is here. Well regarded. He and Silver disagree violently, and often. Or rather, did."

"You know, Emma is a very attractive woman. I can imagine . . ." Jason said.

"Someone wanting to get rid of the husband so they could move in. As it were."

"Well, yeah. I mean, it's been known to happen."

Marcus thought about that and they rode for a while in silence. Then Marcus dropped Jason in front of his house. "You sure you don't want to come for dinner? You can bring Zach, if he puts on clothes."

Jason smiled and said, "Thanks, but Zach only eats when other appetites have been satisfied."

Marcus laughed. "When do you leave for Big Bear?"

"I'll see Emma on Monday morning, and then we'll probably be off."

"Okay, well, have a good time. Try to spend a little time outside."

Jason guffawed and watched Marcus drive away.

13

When he got home, Bob was in the kitchen whipping up something delicious-smelling, and Anna was on the floor of the living room playing with Zelda. Their work papers were still spread all over the dining room table in piles.

"How was the widow?" Bob called from the kitchen.

Marcus walked up behind him and hugged him. "She was . . . something else. Not what I expected."

"They never are. At least, not the interesting ones."

Marcus smiled. "When do we eat? And where's Lily?"

"In about forty minutes. She's playing cards with Cathy at her house. I think Jay really did turn our daughter into a card shark."

Marcus smiled and walked back into the dining room. "I'll set the table. Is it all right if I move your stuff?"

Bob and Anna cried out "No" at exactly the same time.

"Um, I guess we'll eat in the kitchen."

Lily came home, announcing she had trounced Cathy at gin. They ate a lobster casserole and salad, with an apple tart for dessert, and then Bob and Anna went back to work. Lily and Marcus played gin on the kitchen table until Lily's bedtime. Lily won every hand.

The next day, Sunday, they drove up to Laguna Beach to see Ruth. Carol, Little Ruthie, and Jay were there from Los Angeles, but not Alex.

"He's meeting with some Kerry people," Carol explained. John Kerry, the Massachusetts senator, was running for president, and Alex was apparently backing him. The Iowa caucuses and the first primaries were all coming up. Bob's brother had been involved in Democratic party politics for a long time. He had hoped someday to run for local office himself.

"Does he really want to go back to DC?" Bob asked. Alex had done a brief stint in the Clinton Justice Department, working on a special project, flying back and forth to LA. It made Carol's life hellish at home when he was away, with Ruthie tiny, Jay still young. And Alex hated the long commute and the constant jet lag.

Carol sighed. "Apparently."

Bob was about to say more when Lily asked if anyone wanted to play gin.

"Okay," Jay said, "but only if you let me win this time."

Lily laughed. Ruthie sat next to her brother as they played, leaning against him, watching. Seeing Ruthie and Jay together always made Bob and Marcus wonder if they were short-changing Lily in some way by having only one child, but they had talked about it and agreed that they couldn't handle another.

The adults went into the kitchen to make lunch, including Ruth's borscht, Bob's favorite thing, which they ate out on the patio in the warm sun. The cold snap had finally ended. Then Jay took Lily and Ruthie for a long walk on the beach while the adults sat in the living room with coffee. They could hear Jay laughing and the girls squealing.

"I wonder," Ruth said, "if you should put your foot down with Alex. I mean, another commute from LA to DC is just nuts. And very hard on you. Of course, Kerry could lose, so it might not be an issue."

"Oh, I already have put my foot down. I told him either we move there for however long, or nothing. Ruthie is young enough, she'd be fine in school there for a year or two or even four, if it came to that, and Jay is in college, so that wouldn't be a problem. And we could sublet the LA house."

"How did he take it?" Bob asked.

"He agreed. Reluctantly, but he agreed."

"Good," Ruth said, sitting back in her chair.

Bob hesitated, but brought up something that had been on his mind.

"Mom, have you thought about whether you'll stay here? In this house, I mean."

"Yes. I will. For as long as I can. It's home. I have friends here. I love the ocean. Your father knew what he was doing finance-wise, it won't be a problem. But. . ."

"But?" Bob suddenly felt a pang of worry.

"I'm getting a dog."

"Oh!" It was the one thing Bob regretted about his childhood—that they never had a dog.

"What kind?" Carol asked.

"Not sure yet. I've been to the pound a few times. Or maybe a breeder's dog, a Golden, like Zelda and Sam. They're so sweet."

Sam was Alex and Carol's Golden Retriever.

"They're not watchdogs, though, Goldens," Bob said. "Maybe a breed that could offer some protection?"

"Yes, I thought about that."

They talked about different breeds, then about politics— Ruth said she was liking Howard Dean more than Kerry—and then about this and that, with the sun streaming through the windows that overlooked the beach. The windows were open and they could hear the waves. The kids came in from their walk and they all played several rounds of Monopoly. Lily wanted to play cards.

"Oh, no. I'm not falling for that again," Jay said. Ruth brought out all the board games.

They ordered pizza for dinner with a big salad and then said their good-byes.

"Grandma, come visit us," Lily said at the front door, giving Ruth a long hug. Bob saw that his mother had a tear in her eye.

14

Monday and Tuesday were work days for both Bob and Marcus, Bob at the office, Marcus at home, trying to finish his article, Zelda at his feet in his study when she wasn't demanding attention or a walk, which was once every hour like clockwork.

Jason came over for dinner Tuesday night and filled them in on the Silver investigation; Zach had twisted his ankle as soon as they hit the slopes at Big Bear, so they came home.

"I know he looks like a tough marine, but he's a marshmallow inside," Jason said, sighing.

Jason had spoken to Maggie Garner that afternoon on the UCSD campus. He brought it up after Lily had gone to her room after dinner and the adults lingered over coffee.

"She hemmed and hawed, but eventually she pointed me toward this Isaacson guy. Apparently he and Silver were really at each other's throats about this new research center. How it should be organized, who would lead it."

"That doesn't surprise me," Marcus said.

"And there seems to be a lot of money at stake at that center. They just got a $25 million bequest, with more on the horizon."

"Wow. That could be motive, right there," Bob said.

"Maybe," Jason said.

"She also showed me some angry email exchanges between them. Some of them really were over the top. On both sides."

"Remember, though, academic egos. They're huge. Both Isaacson and Silver had them," Marcus added. He liked Isaacson, to the extent that he knew him, and had a hard time believing he'd committed murder. Culturally, Isaacson was the polar opposite of Chuck Silver—rumpled and a bit of a slob, everyone thought. He kept a low profile, but he was a solid scholar and a nice guy.

"So she thinks Isaacson could have done it?" Bob asked, ignoring Marcus.

"Well, she also mentioned this guy Templeton at UCLA. And I did get the feeling . . ."

Marcus's face asked the question.

"I got the feeling she'd prefer it be Templeton, since he's an outsider. Less bad publicity."

"That doesn't surprise me. I mean, reputation matters. One professor murdering another on the same campus isn't exactly the image they're going for. But . . ."

"But?"

"It's hard for me to imagine any professor murdering another in cold blood, no matter how much they fought. It just doesn't feel like it's in our DNA."

"It's in anyone's DNA," Bob said, "under the right circumstances. Anyone can snap. Anyone." Bob had seen enough murder cases to know what he was talking about, Marcus knew. Not that he was jaded, but he had become more and more realistic about human nature as he went through case after case. More realistic and more pessimistic.

Jason agreed. "Meek little housewives, kids, you name it. Anyone can turn into a murderer."

"Is there evidence against Isaacson?" Marcus asked.

"The police have already interviewed him. And, I found out, his DNA was found at the murder scene."

"That's not a surprise," Marcus said. "He was on campus, in and out of that building, all the time. That doesn't prove anything."

"I know," Jason said. "But it's convenient if they want a quick arrest. There's a lot of pressure, apparently, to wrap this up quickly. Pressure from Oakland, even Sacramento."

The central University of California administration was in Oakland, up in the Bay Area, and the University system, with its ten campuses, had many friends in the state capital. UC had been a major engine of California's growth, especially, lately, in engineering, medicine, and biotech. More than most state universities elsewhere in the country, it exercised real political power.

"I need to go up and interview this Templeton. Marcus, I'd like you to come with me."

Marcus frowned. "I don't know. I hate getting so involved. How would we explain my being there?"

"I talked to Emma about it. I wanted her permission to involve you in any interviews with academic types. She was all for it. We can say she asked you to sit in. That should do it."

Marcus looked at Bob.

"Don't look at me, it's not my case," Bob said.

"Please, Marcus," Jason said. "I'm at sea in your world. I'm barely literate. I need your help."

Marcus got up to fetch the coffee pot from the kitchen. He really didn't want to do this, but he didn't think he could say no. Emma was a colleague, Jason a close friend who had done innumerable favors for Bob and Marcus over the years.

"Okay."

"Thanks. I'll owe you."

Marcus tried to smile.

15

Wednesday, New Year's Eve, was a lovely, warm day. In the morning Bob and Marcus took Lily to the San Diego zoo, which she loved—along with all the animals except the tigers.

"I'm afraid of them," she'd said timidly the first time they were there, and that never seemed to change.

At the nearby San Diego Art Museum they looked around a bit, had lunch on the terrace, and afterward strolled through Balboa Park. In the afternoon everyone relaxed at home. Lily took a long nap so she could stay up until midnight. She was excited about a new year and loved watching it on TV, which they had let her do the year before for the first time.

That evening they had been invited to a party at the home of Jim and Arlene Stewart, old friends; Jim was now emeritus at UCSD. Cathy wasn't available and Jason volunteered to baby sit, which surprised them.

"Where's Zach tonight?"

"Don't ask." They didn't.

The party was crowded with scores of university folks. Everyone was dressed up and the Stewarts had hung streamers and balloons all over their house and a big banner in the living room saying "Welcome to 2004!" Maggie Garner put in an appearance with her dour husband George, an accountant, but they didn't stay long. Lucy Boynton, the local state Representative, put in an appearance as well . . . talking up John Kerry to anyone who would listen.

Marcus greeted various colleagues, introduced Bob to those who hadn't met him. There were many new faculty members there; UCSD was growing fast and hiring constantly. Jim and Arlene had functioned as a kind of informal welcoming committee for decades. They had been especially welcoming to Bob and Marcus when they first arrived.

Lots of people talked about Chuck Silver. What a loss he was, how much he had accomplished. Several younger faculty talked about how much he had helped them in all sorts of ways, writing letters for grants, securing access to manuscript collections, making introductions to people they needed to know to get ahead in their particular subfield. One young woman had tears in her eyes as she talked about all Silver had done for her.

It was a revelation to Marcus. He had had friendly conversations and an occasional lunch with Chuck, and Chuck had written one or two letters of recommendation for him, but Marcus never thought of him as a particularly generous type, or as someone who took a strong interest in the careers of his younger colleagues. But apparently he did.

Listening to people talk about his generosity, Marcus felt a pang of guilt for not having gotten to know him better. But Chuck was so famous and so busy, Marcus had assumed he just didn't have time for mentoring. Clearly, he was wrong.

At one point Marcus looked over and saw Bob talking to a tall young man he didn't recognize. He was lean, blond, and gave off a gay vibe, and at one point put his hand on Bob's arm. They both were laughing.

When Bob turned around, just before midnight, he was smiling.

He came and found Marcus, and everyone counted down to midnight and then sang "Auld Lang Syne," which Marcus always thought silly—it was an old Scottish song, and no one really knew what the words meant or where they came from. But they both sang along, and then kissed.

In the car on the way home, Marcus asked Bob if he had a good time.

"I did, better than I thought I would."

"Who was that blond guy?"

"Hmm? Derrick something-or-other. An economist. New. From Stanford, by way of Harvard. Apparently once worked at Treasury. A real snob."

"Family?" Marcus asked, using then-current code for "gay."

"If he isn't, he's certainly open to persuasion."

Marcus laughed.

At home they found Jason sitting in front of a fire, looking pensive and a bit sad. They sat with him for a while and drank from a pot of mint tea he had made. Jason seemed reluctant to leave but finally got up; it was past 2 a.m.

"Thanks for staying with Lily," Bob said as Jason put on his jacket.

"Any time. You guys are so lucky, she's an amazing kid. Even though she beat me at gin four times."

16

After a quiet New Year's Day and weekend, normal life resumed. Bob and Anna worked hard on a complex divorce case that also involved assault and battery; Marcus prepared for and then

52   —•— **H. N. Hirsch** —•—

began Winter quarter. Lily went back to school. Jason was busy wrapping up a few other cases. The weather was sunny and slightly cool during the day, cold at night, a typical January. The rain, if it came at all in San Diego, came in February or March.

Soon word reached them that the police had arrested Fred Isaacson for Chuck Silver's murder. In addition to his emails, they had uncovered witnesses. One had seen them in a heated argument at the MLA the morning Chuck was killed, and another placed him on campus and in the building right before the murder. After arraignment and release on a $2 million bond, he hired Sarah Kruks, a high-priced defense attorney whom Bob knew, though not well.

The story dominated the local news for a few days. Isaacson pleaded not guilty and a trial date was set for April.

Emma summoned Jason and Marcus to a meeting at her home the day after Isaacson's arrest; they met in the late afternoon after Marcus had spent the day on campus. Emma looked much better, and younger, than she had in their previous meetings. Whatever shock she had been feeling at the time of the murder seemed to have worn off.

"What do you make of the arrest?" she asked as soon as Marcus and Jason had sat down.

"It's a weak case," Jason offered. "All the evidence is circumstantial. No real witness, no murder weapon. Isaacson being on campus that day is not surprising."

"That's my impression as well," Emma said. "I mean, Fred and Chuck fought about a lot of things, including this new research center, but it was a good-natured rivalry. I can't see Fred doing this. I mean, my God, he had been a dinner guest here. Several times. He always struck me as a kind man. Perhaps with a bit of a temper . . . which Chuck had as well."

"Did the police interview you about Fred?" Marcus asked.

"No." Her voice carried a note of surprise, shared by both of the men.

"I'd like you to continue investigating," Emma said. She sounded resolute.

"All right, I can do that," Jason said. "Have you remembered anything that might be useful?"

"Nothing beyond what I've already told you. I wish I could give you more."

After they left, Marcus asked Jason why the police would have arrested Isaacson with so little evidence.

"Political pressure. My sources say intense pressure. It happens."

"But if they can't make the charges stick, why would the DA bring charges?"

"The pressure is to arrest someone, get the story out of the headlines. That's the goal. The public feels reassured and forgets about the case. Then what happens later doesn't matter so much. Usually."

Marcus understood; he had seen and heard enough from Bob's cases to know that this sort of thing, arresting and trying people on weak evidence, went on far too often.

"So what do we do now?"

"We begin interviewing other possible suspects. I've made contact with Templeton in Los Angeles. We should start with him."

"In cases like this, have you ever uncovered the real criminal after the police arrest the wrong guy?" Marcus asked.

"Yeah. A few times. A couple of times when I worked for Bob."

"How's Zach?" Marcus asked after a few minutes.

"Gone. Like all of them," Jason said. There was a note of regret in Jason's voice, something Marcus couldn't remember hearing before.

17

They arranged to interview Templeton the following Friday in Los Angeles. They'd drive up on Friday morning. Bob would pick up Ruth in Laguna Beach later, after Lily finished school, and they'd all spend the night with Alex and Carol.

Templeton was renting a house in the Troutsdale Estates from a UCLA faculty member on leave. It was a huge white stucco thing with the requisite pool, surrounded by lush greenery, at the edge of a canyon. Marcus had been in Southern California long enough to know that while beautiful, all the greenery posed a fire hazard. It seemed like some part of LA was always on fire in the late summer or early fall.

They rang the doorbell at 1 p.m., as arranged, and a distinguished looking man of fifty-five or so opened the door. He was dressed casually but carefully in a gray cashmere sweater, pleated wool slacks, and tasseled loafers without socks.

"Shall we sit on the patio?" he asked in an impeccable British accent. "It's such a lovely day. I've been gorging on the California sun."

They arranged themselves around a patio table, under an umbrella, and a maid appeared and brought out coffee and biscuits on a tray.

"So, gentlemen, am I a suspect in the murder of Chuck Silver? I believe an arrest has been made."

"Yes, it has," Jason said, "but we don't believe the police have arrested the right person."

"And why is that?" Templeton sipped his coffee. "And who is 'we'"?

"For one thing, the evidence is weak, and entirely circumstantial. And Emma Baker wants to find the person responsible."

"I see. And what explains your presence here, Professor George?"

Before Marcus could speak, Jason responded. "Ms. Baker asked Marcus to help me in the investigation, since I have so little experience with your world."

"Ah. Yes, it's true, we live in a strange habitat."

Marcus smiled and nodded and sipped his coffee. He felt awkward beyond belief.

"We've been told," Jason went on, "that you and Professor Silver argued at a conference session the day he died. It's been described as a quite heated exchange."

Both Jason and Marcus watched Templeton's reaction closely. He didn't seem the least bit ruffled or anxious. He even smiled as if reminiscing.

"Yes, that's true. It was at a session on Arabic literature. I think Silver's take on the subject is completely wrong. But—"

He stopped to sip. "But that's not news. I've been saying the same thing for a long while. We've tangled, intellectually, for many years, in print, at conferences. We're both known for our positions."

"You were seen leaving the session together."

"Yes. We went and had a drink, and continued talking."

"And what happened after that?"

"I drove back here."

"Were you alone?" The crucial question. Jason tried to sound casual.

"No, two graduate students were in the car with me, I had given them a ride down. I can give you their names."

"Yes, that would be helpful. And you drove straight back to Los Angeles?"

"Yes. It was fairly early in the afternoon, on a weekend, and we wanted to avoid rush hour traffic, which, as I've discovered, is murderous." At the mention of murder, Templeton smiled. Somewhat sadistically, Marcus thought.

"Did you have an affair with Emma Baker?" Always try to

throw the witness off base, mix the important questions with the routine, Bob had once said. Jason clearly knew how to do this sort of thing.

"Yes."

Again, no hesitation, no sign of emotion. If this is British sangfroid, Marcus thought, it's working.

"When?"

"Before she married Silver. It began when she was working in archives in London."

"Did you see Mrs. Baker at the MLA?"

"Yes. We had lunch. Thursday."

"And did you attempt to revive your relationship at that lunch?"

"Yes, I did." Again, complete composure, with a slight smile.

"And?"

"And she politely declined. As you colonials like to say, win some, lose some."

"I don't believe we've been colonials for about two hundred years. Do you know Professor Isaacson, who's been accused of the murder?"

"We've met. But I don't really know him."

"So you know nothing that could clarify his relationship with Silver?"

"No, I'm afraid not."

"Can you think of anyone who would want Professor Silver dead?"

"No. That I can't do. That is, he had intellectual enemies, but then we all do. I'm sure Professor George can vouch for that."

Marcus nodded. He was beginning to feel like Vanna White on *Wheel of Fortune*.

"Well," Jason said, "thank you for being so forthright. If we could get the names of those graduate students who drove with you, we can leave you in peace."

"Of course." Templeton went into the house and emerged a few minutes later, handing Jason a slip of elegant stationery.

They shook hands at the door.

In the car, they looked at each other.

"Either he's been studying Cary Grant movies," Jason said, "or he's made of ice."

18

Jason dropped Marcus at Alex and Carol's house in Santa Monica. It was around 3:00, and Ruthie soon came home from school.

"Uncle Marcus!" she said, hugging him.

They sat out on the patio and enjoyed the sun and the breeze coming in from the ocean, even though it was a bit chilly. Their Golden Retriever, Samson, cuddled with Ruthie on the grass.

Around 5:00, Bob, Lily, and Ruth arrived, and an hour later Alex came home. Ruth and Bob cooked—roast chicken, tabouli, baby red-skin potatoes—while the other adults drank wine or tonic water in the living room. Lily and Ruthie were giggling upstairs.

"So," Alex said over dinner to Marcus, "catch the killer yet?"

"Alex!" Ruth scolded good-naturedly.

"Honestly, I don't know what I'm doing in the middle of this thing. But the widow seems to want me involved."

Lily and Ruthie looked puzzled but didn't ask any questions. Marcus suddenly felt a bit embarrassed for using the word "widow" in front of Ruth, but she didn't blink.

She steered the conversation to politics. "Alex, are you sure Kerry is the one?"

"Yes. He's a veteran. He was a critic of Vietnam. He has credibility when he criticizes this disaster in Iraq."

"He's just so. . . ." Ruth hesitated.

"Stiff," Carol offered.

"Yes. And boring," Marcus added.

Bob nodded. "And you would really go back to DC?" he asked his brother.

"I don't know. Maybe. That's way down the road."

Bob poured himself more wine, a third glass. Ruth glanced at Marcus. He noticed too.

The next morning, after pancakes, Bob and Marcus drove home; Bob had work to do on his case with Anna. Ruth and Lily stayed. Alex said he'd drive Ruth home on Sunday and then Ruth would drive Lily down to San Diego Sunday evening.

Bob was driving.

"Bobby," Marcus said. "I need to talk to you about something." Since they were alone, it seemed like the right time.

"Hmm?"

"Ruth has noticed you've been drinking more. She mentioned it to me. To be honest, I've noticed it too."

Bob didn't say anything for a long while. He looked straight ahead.

"Maybe I have been. I mean, Jesus, my father died. Out of nowhere. And work is hellish right now."

"And you're turning forty."

Bob nodded.

"I understand," Marcus said. "And I'm sure Ruth does too. It's just we don't want it to become a problem. If you think you need help . . ."

"I don't," Bob said, firmly.

"Okay. Don't be mad. Please."

"I'm not mad. Really. But it's not a problem." He turned toward Marcus and smiled.

Marcus dropped the subject. He didn't know what else to say.

19

On Monday, Jason called and asked Marcus to set up meetings with Julie Klein and Ed Peterson, the other likely suspects. He did, although he had a hard time explaining to each of them why he was involved. Peterson, especially, seemed reluctant to meet, but Marcus persuaded him. Both said they had already spoken to the police and had nothing more to say. Marcus emphasized that he was working with a private investigator at Emma's request.

"The police can bungle an investigation like this," Marcus told both of them. "My partner is a lawyer, I've seen it happen. The case against Fred is really weak. Even I can see that."

He arranged the meeting with Julie for Friday and with Peterson for the beginning of the following week.

Meanwhile, Jason reported, he visited the apartment at Tourmaline and said he didn't find any clues, although the place, he said, was a one-bedroom apartment and could easily have been used for trysts. The bedroom had a lived-in look. The living room was just a large desk, a file cabinet, and a comfortable chair and ottoman, with lots of books scattered around, several open on the desk.

Jason also was looking into Chuck's finances and the estate, and, so far, had found nothing suspicious. There was a large trust fund for Chloe and everything else was left to Emma, with a clause stating that the remainder of the estate would go into Chloe's trust if Emma remarried. Jason said that was somewhat old-fashioned, but not really unusual.

Marcus thought that was a strange provision. "Do husbands put that there to discourage the wife from remarrying?"

"You can look at it that way, yes."

They met Julie Klein in Marcus's office on campus on Friday morning. Marcus was fidgety and really did not want to be there, but Jason insisted. Julie was still his graduate student, and he knew Jason would ask highly personal questions. Marcus was scrupulous about not getting involved in students' personal lives, ever since one of his students had been found to be a murderer ten years before. If a student tried to talk to him about personal issues, he cut them off as gently as he could and offered to help them find professional help if they needed it.

Julie had dressed up for the meeting; she was wearing a dress and high heels and make-up, and it looked like she had had her blond hair styled into a French bun. Marcus realized for the first time that she was a very attractive young woman.

Jason started by explaining why Emma was investigating, his role, and so forth. Julie nodded. She was clearly nervous.

Jason started with soft questions, how long she had known Professor Silver, how often they met, his role vis-a-vis her dissertation, and other innocuous subjects. He took notes.

"When was the last time you saw Professor Silver?"

"I ran into him in the hallway at the MLA. I actually missed his session on Friday because it conflicted with another panel, and I knew what he was likely to say."

"I'm sorry to have to ask this, but did your relationship with Professor Silver extend beyond the professional?"

Well, Marcus thought, at least he put it delicately.

Julie looked down at her hands for a long time.

"Yes."

She glanced at Marcus, who did his best to keep his face neutral.

"How long had it been going on?"

"About a year. A bit longer."

"Where did you meet?"

"At his apartment in Pacific Beach."

"How often?"

"It varied. Not terribly often, lately. I suppose it averaged out to two times a month. More at the beginning."

"And it was completely consensual on your part? He did not pressure you into the affair?"

Julie seemed upset for the first time. "Yes, completely consensual. In fact, I'd say I was the more aggressive party, at the beginning."

Of course, Marcus thought, she could just be saying that. There was no way to really know. But if it was true, he was a bit shocked.

"So your feelings about him were positive? He hadn't tried to end the affair or anything of that sort?"

"No." She paused for a moment and fiddled with her purse strap. "No." She looked at Jason. "Am I a murder suspect now?"

"No. We're just gathering facts. But, can you tell us, where were you on the Friday afternoon Professor Silver died?"

"I was at the convention in the morning. Then I went home."

"Can anyone confirm that?"

She shifted her legs.

"My roommate." Jason asked for names and scribbled them down.

"Is there anything else?" Julie asked.

"No. Thank you for being so forthcoming. And please understand, these questions were necessary. We will keep as much confidential as we can."

With all the sarcasm she could muster, she replied as she stood up.

"Yes. Of course." She gave Marcus a dirty look as she left.

20

Jason threw his notepad down on Marcus's desk and immediately sat down and crossed his arms. He seemed more frustrated than angry, but Marcus picked up the mood.

"We're not getting anywhere, are we?" he asked.

"No. Everyone has alibis. So far. But it's early for an investigation of this sort."

"Maybe the police have the guy who did it? I mean, it's possible, isn't it?" Marcus tried to sound hopeful.

"Yeah, possible. But my gut says no. Too rushed, too circumstantial. Weak case. Very."

"Have you talked to the police?"

"Once or twice. They're not telling me much. They never do in situations like this."

Marcus frowned. "What about Emma's list? The other women she suspects."

"Right, we have to start talking to them. And to the names on the second list, the professionals." Jason took it out. "Who on here do you know?"

Marcus told him, and Jason wrote a little "M" next to those names.

Jason got up. "Okay. I'll leave you to think great thoughts, or whatever it is you guys do here in the Ivory Tower."

Marcus laughed. He turned his attention to the work on his desk.

After Jason left, Marcus had a sudden, disturbing thought, seemingly out of nowhere.

What if Emma really was responsible for the murder?

Chuck's estate was substantial. He played around. Maybe Emma was just making up the "I gave him his space" narrative. Maybe she hated his cheating.

That afternoon Marcus called Jason and asked him about it.

"I thought of that too, but there'd be a cash trail, and there isn't. She would have had to pay someone to do it. I looked carefully. Absolutely no sign of that kind of transaction. Unless they kept something like $100,000 cash in a safe or safe deposit box somewhere, there's just no evidence of that. And they were well off, but not so well off that they would keep that much money lying around. It would be stupid. Most of the wealth came from Chuck's family and was fairly well tied up. Sophisticated investments. Their salaries were deposited into a joint checking account like clockwork and used to pay operating expenses."

"Well," Marcus said, "it was just a thought."

After his afternoon class, Maggie Garner's secretary called and said Maggie wanted to see him.

"Would 4:00 be convenient?"

Marcus closed his eyes. "Yes, I can be there." He had been hoping to leave the office early. He wanted to go home and play with Zelda and Lily when she got home from school. Anything to take his mind off murder.

The UCSD administrative complex was a set of low, wooden structures separated by covered walkways. Marcus made his way there just before his appointment, and he was kept waiting until 4:40, when a secretary ushered him into the inner office.

Maggie Garner did not apologize for keeping him waiting. When he was ushered into her office, she was taking a Diet Coke out of a small refrigerator; she didn't offer him one, nor did she smile or say hello.

"Marcus. Tell me. Why are you involved in the investigation of Chuck's murder?"

"You know why, Maggie. Because you summoned me to meet with Emma, along with Bob. Our friend Jason Thompson is doing the investigation. Jason asked me to sit in on interviews with university types, since he knows so little about how we operate. I'm not happy doing it, but he thinks it necessary." He could feel anger rising in his chest.

"I don't think it's appropriate."

"Well then, Maggie, you shouldn't have brought me and my partner into the situation to begin with. Am I violating any University rules?"

"No, not really. Just raising eyebrows."

"So does murder."

Maggie smiled a brittle smile. She sipped her drink. "I'd like you to suggest to Emma that she call off the investigation. An arrest has been made. She should let the process play itself out."

"Maggie, you should speak to her yourself, if that's what you think."

"Marcus, I'm ordering you to talk to her about this."

"I beg your pardon?"

"I think you heard me." She took a long drink from her can of soda.

Marcus paused for a long moment. He kept his voice as calm as he could manage. "You don't have that authority, Maggie." He looked unwaveringly at her, staring her in the eye. "So there are two options here." He took a breath before continuing. "You can rescind this 'order' and apologize, or I will file a complaint against you with Privilege and Tenure."

Marcus had once served on that committee, which dealt with any faculty member's complaint against the University, or any accusation by the University against a faculty member. Marcus had had to participate in a particularly gruesome investigation of research fraud at UCSD's medical school, which, he learned, was a cesspool of ego—and large federal grants.

Maggie turned red and said nothing. After a moment she turned to the computer table behind her desk and looked at her schedule. "You'll have to excuse me, I have to get to another meeting."

"By all means." He got up and left.

21

When Marcus got back to his office, his heart was pounding and the phone was ringing. It was Maggie.

"Marcus, I'm sorry. I should not have used that word. It's been a hellish day. Hellish month, really. Let's say I'm asking you to speak to Emma about this."

"No, Maggie, I will not. You got me into this. If you want to tell her something, please do it yourself."

He hung up without waiting for a reply. He was angry, more angry than he could remember being for a long time. He stood up and paced around the office.

Lots of faculty members said Maggie Garner could be—in the words of one of his colleagues—a first-class bitch, but he had never experienced her that way. "Imperious" was the word most often used to describe her. She even used an undergraduate to keep watch over her designated parking space in front of her office; apparently, someone had parked there. Once.

He gathered his things and drove home.

The drive calmed him, as did finding Lily, Cathy, and Zelda playing in the back yard. There was a message on the answering machine from Bob saying he'd have to work late.

"Pop is going to be late, so we'll order pizza," he announced. "Cathy, you're welcome to stay."

Lily called Bob "Pop" and Marcus "Dad."

"Why do you get to be 'Pop'?" Marcus asked when Lily first called him that.

"Because I'm the cool one," Bob replied.

"Yay, pizza! Stay, Cathy. Please." Lily tugged at the sitter.

"No, I should go, I've got homework," she said. She hugged Lily and Marcus walked her to the door.

"You look awful," she said at the front door. "Hard day?"

"Yes." He tried to smile and Cathy patted his arm. He went back to the yard.

"Come on," he said to Lily. "What kind of pizza do you want? Do you have any homework?"

"I did it already."

Lily announced she wanted the vegetarian special from their local pizza place, which Marcus ordered, knowing it would take about an hour to arrive. He fed Zelda and turned on the news. Lily snuggled next to him on the couch while he watched, Zelda at their feet, and he began to relax.

After dinner, the phone rang. It was Anna, Bob's law partner.

"Marcus, Bob had an accident. He fell and hit his head. He's all right, I took him to the hospital in Hillcrest. But they want to keep him overnight for observation." She told him where he'd be. "I'll stay until you get here."

Marcus felt panic rising but managed to stay outwardly calm, not wanting to alarm Lily. He called Cathy from the phone in the bedroom and said it was an emergency, he needed her to come back. She arrived in ten minutes and Marcus explained what had happened.

"I've got to go out, pumpkin," he said to Lily. "Be good."

"I'm always good," Lily said laughing.

He drove to the hospital, trying hard not to imagine the worst. He told himself, over and over, to stay calm. It wasn't working.

He found Bob in a private room, Anna at his side. He looked slightly dazed and had a small bandage on the back of his head, but he smiled.

He leaned over and patted Bob's hand, and smelled whiskey on his breath.

Anna said she'd be going. They both thanked her.

After she had gone, Marcus pulled up a chair.

"So, how do you feel?"

"Slight headache. Not bad really." He smiled again.

"How did it happen?"

"It's silly, really. We were working in the conference room and I got up to get some papers I had left in my office. My feet hurt, I had taken my shoes off, I was in my stocking feet. Somehow I slipped. I guess the floor had just been waxed. I caught the corner of the conference table. It just needed a few stitches. It should be fine. They just want to make sure there's no concussion or anything like that."

Marcus nodded and forced himself to smile.

"I wasn't drunk, if that's what you're thinking. I had a very tiny nip with a sandwich. That's all. They checked my blood alcohol level. It's really low."

Marcus had to make a split-second decision. He decided now was not the time to press.

He smiled. "Good."

A nurse came in to check Bob's vitals, and a kind-looking orderly brought a disgusting-looking dinner of beef stew, which Bob hardly touched.

"What time will they release you tomorrow?"

"I'm not sure. Early, I hope. I have a ton of work."

"Call me first thing, let me know what's what."

"Will do."

For a while they watched the national news. Bob kept closing his eyes.

"I should get home," Marcus said around 9:00. "Explain things to Lily before she goes to bed. She'll be worried when you don't come home."

"Yes, go. I'll be fine. I just need to sleep."

They kissed.

He stopped at the nurse's station and asked for an update. The nurse said it was not a deep cut, and they were just being cautious. They didn't really suspect anything, and they had done a scan of his brain. No sign of a brain bleed, which would have been the dangerous thing.

"We'll do another scan in the morning, just to be safe. Then we'll discharge him."

On the drive home, Marcus wondered if he had ever had a worse day. He had, he was sure, but at the moment, he couldn't think of when.

22

When he got home, he thanked Cathy again and put Lily to bed. He decided to tell Lily at least a little of the truth. She was alarmed, but just a little, which impressed Marcus. She really was growing up.

"Really, he'll be fine. They're just being extra careful." Lily nodded.

After he turned out Lily's light, he hesitated for a long time, but then called Anna at home, and asked her to meet him for an early breakfast.

He hardly slept. He kept reaching over to Bob's side of the bed.

They met at 8:00 am at the Crest Café in Hillcrest, after Bob had gotten Lily off to school. He apologized for asking Anna to inform on her partner.

"I get it. You're worried about his drinking."

"Yes."

"It's true, it has picked up since his dad died."

"I know. I tried talking to him about it, but he said it wasn't a problem."

"I'm not sure it is. I just noticed an uptick. Not a huge uptick, but some."

"Did he really slip in his stocking feet?"

"Yes. And the floor had just been waxed."

Well, Marcus thought, *he's telling the truth.* That was a relief.

"We had sandwiches," Anna went on. "From the deli down the street. And Bob had a really small gulp of scotch. I did too. Not enough to make anyone drunk."

Anna looked uncomfortable, but she went on. "He keeps a bottle in his desk. He has for a long time."

Marcus knew that was true.

"He would only take a drink when we won a case. We both would. But he's been dipping into it a little more. If we stay late."

"Has he ever appeared drunk? I hate myself for asking, but . . ."

"I understand. I would be asking the same question. No, never. And he never drinks before a court appearance, or an important meeting. I would notice, we whisper to each other in court or at depositions. I'd know."

Marcus felt relieved, but still uneasy.

"I think turning forty is getting to him." Anna had been invited to the party, which was coming up.

"Well, it's a big one," Marcus said.

"It hits everyone, from what I can see. And on top of his dad's death . . ."

"Yeah. It's a lot. I wish I knew how to support him more."

"You do support him. He's said it many times. He would be lost without you."

"Thank you. Thank you for saying that."

Anna put her hand on top of his.

"He'll get through this. You both will."

Marcus wondered what they would do without Anna. She was super smart with pure common sense, like Ruth, like Carol. He wondered, not for the first time, if women had cornered the market on that personality type.

23

Marcus felt better after breakfast, and, since it was close by, went straight to the hospital. He was having a brain scan, a nurse said; Marcus waited in the room.

Bob walked back in, smiling, about thirty minutes later. He dressed in the clothes he'd worn the day before and looked like his old self.

"They're letting me go. No sign of anything," he said, clearly in a good mood. He leaned down and kissed Marcus on the lips.

"Ah. Good. Let's go home."

They took care of the paperwork at the nurse's desk and left.

Bob was clearly happy to be home. Zelda was beside herself. Bob showered, changed his bandage, put on fresh clothes, and said he was heading to the office.

"Maybe you should take it easy today," Marcus said, hopefully.

"I'm fine. The doctor said it's okay to go back to work. It's just a cut."

"Okay. But don't put in too long a day."

Bob looked skeptical.

"Really. You've had a shock."

They kissed goodbye, and both headed out the front door. Marcus drove to campus feeling relieved. He listened to the local classical station on the way, parked, and then the phone rang almost as soon as he settled in his office.

It was Jason, to tell him they had an interview that afternoon at 4:30 with Mona Sayers, one of the women on Emma's list, who was a post-doctoral fellow in the Physics Department. They'd meet in her office.

Marcus sighed but agreed to be there. He prepped and then taught his class and spent some time reading a colleague's newest paper. He skipped lunch; he had eaten too much pizza the night before and felt bloated.

Sayers turned out to be a stunning thirty-something redhead, working on water desalinization. They found her in one of the new, ugly concrete engineering buildings. In her dark blue pantsuit and very high heels, she reminded Marcus of a young Lucille Ball.

She told them she had met Chuck Silver at a party.

"And you started an affair?" Jason asked.

"Yes. Chuck said it wasn't a problem for his wife. I took him at his word."

"How often did you meet?"

She thought for a moment. "Not very often, maybe once a month."

"Where would you get together?"

"His apartment near the beach, or at my place. The place I'm renting, up in Del Mar."

"Do you have any idea who would want to do him harm?"

"No. I was completely shocked to hear he had been shot. He was a sweet man, a teddy bear."

"For the record, where were you on Friday, December 27?"

"I spent that week with my parents in Denver. I always spend Christmas with them."

"Just to be thorough, could we get their phone number?"

"Yes of course." She jotted it down on a piece of paper.

Jason thanked her for her time.

"No problem. I hope you find out who did this. No one on campus seems to think the guy they arrested is guilty."

"Short and sweet," Marcus said as they left the building.

"And useless. A teddy bear. Who got murdered. Someone must have wanted him dead."

Marcus had a thought. "Is there any chance this was random? A thief?"

"What was there to steal in that mailroom?"

"Well, nothing. Unless they wanted his cash or his watch or something. He did have the air of a rich man. Maybe someone just followed him into the building."

"No, I checked. That's the first thing the police always think of. His wallet was on him when they police found him, with lots of cash. So was his watch. Nothing was missing."

Marcus frowned.

"I promised Emma I'd stop over, give her a progress report," Jason said. "Except of course there's been no progress. Can you make it?"

"Um, no. I should get home, check on Bob."

"Why, what's wrong?"

Marcus briefly told him the story.

"It's turning forty, I bet," Jason said. "That sent me into a tailspin. If he escapes with just a cut on the head, he'll be lucky. I took up skiing and broke my leg in three places. It's harder for us."

"You mean 'friends of Dorothy'."

"My God, I haven't heard that phrase in ten years," Jason said, laughing.

"Funny, birthdays have never bothered me," Marcus said.

"That's because you found the right guy."

24

Bob was home when Marcus got there and seemed like his old self; he was cooking, Lily was doing homework at the kitchen table, and Zelda was standing next to Bob, hoping for a handout or a dropped piece of food. Everything seemed normal. For the first time in hours—days?—Marcus relaxed.

The following week they attended Chuck's Memorial Service

with Jason. It was held at the large Unitarian Church in Mission Hills, the neighborhood next to Hillcrest. To his surprise, several of Chuck's intellectual adversaries flew in for the service, including Sandra Bernstein from Berkeley, one of his fiercest intellectual foes. Dozens of UCSD faculty and graduate students showed up, and even a few undergraduates. The place was packed and the room overheated quickly.

The speakers all praised Chuck's scholarship, his willingness to take controversial stands, his dedication to his family. Maggie Garner spoke about what a coup it had been to recruit Chuck and what an asset he was to the University. She made him sound like a commodity, which, Marcus had realized soon after arriving, was the way UCSD thought about its faculty—"What's the value-added?" was the question he heard most often in faculty meetings when discussing whom to hire or grant tenure. The phrase always made Marcus wince. More than once he had seen a young scholar tossed out, denied tenure, despite a good record, because the "value added" wasn't judged to be sufficient.

He remembered one conversation in particular, about a tenure case. "His work is good. He did everything he's supposed to do. But he's just not cutting edge." Cutting edge. Value-added. Like a Maserati versus a Corvette, he remembered thinking with distaste.

Emma got up and spoke last. She was wearing a simple black dress and moved slowly. She talked about how much Chuck loved Chloe, who was sitting ramrod straight in the front row, dry-eyed, in a dark gray dress with a pink bow.

"We had his love. Just not enough time," Emma said, finally, looking at Chloe, and then went back to her seat. Many of those listening, Marcus noticed, had tears in their eyes.

The minister, who had been acting as host, thanked everyone for coming and announced there would be a reception in the courtyard. It was a warm, sunny day.

As they got up, Marcus told Jason that Sandra Bernstein was present, and that they should see if they could set up a meeting. Jason nodded.

They made their way across the room to where Bernstein was talking to a group of people Marcus didn't recognize. Bernstein had on perfect funeral clothes: black suit, a gray, almost lavender, silk blouse, and matching earrings and necklace of beautifully faceted onyx beads. Even in 3-inch heels she was surprisingly short. She looked to be around sixty and was at the moment the chair of Berkeley's high-powered Rhetoric Department—a department that many described as a nest of rattlesnakes. In fact, most departments at the school were described that way.

Marcus introduced himself and asked if he could have a private word.

"Yes, of course," she said. They walked over to a quieter spot.

Marcus introduced Jason, and Jason explained their role.

"We were hoping we could speak to you privately about Professor Silver's death" Jason said. "Emma doesn't think the police have arrested the right man, and the case against him is very weak. We're trying to gather as much information about the professor's life as possible."

"I see. I'm staying overnight. I could meet you this afternoon."

She gave them her hotel information and they arranged to meet at 4:00.

Jason thanked her and left the reception. Marcus stayed a bit longer and spoke to a few people before leaving. Emma nodded and smiled a bit at Marcus as he left. Bob had already left for his office; he was due in court.

After teaching his afternoon class, Marcus met Jason in the lobby of Bernstein's glitzy new hotel in downtown San Diego. They had arranged to meet her in the hotel's bar.

She joined them right at 4:00. She had changed into slacks

and flat shoes and looked quite relaxed.

"Thank you for seeing us."

Bernstein nodded. A waiter appeared and Bernstein asked for a glass of chardonnay. Marcus and Jason both asked for mineral water.

"We understand you and Professor Silver had an adversarial intellectual relationship," Jason began.

"Yes, you could say that," she replied. "We disagreed about the politics of the Middle East, especially about Israeli politics."

"And, as I understand it, you had some sharp exchanges, in print and at various conferences."

"Yes, that's true."

"Were you at the conference here in San Diego over the holidays?"

"Yes." She took a sip of her wine. "I don't usually go to the MLA, it's so hard over the holidays, what with family and so forth, but someone I know from Berkeley's English department asked me to appear on a panel. As a favor."

"Was that Professor Silver's panel?"

"No, a different one. But I attended Chuck's panel. I wanted to hear what he had to say. I disagreed with almost everything," she said, very casually.

"Just to be thorough, can you tell us where you were on the afternoon and evening after Professor Silver's panel?"

"Oh, I see," she said after a pause and a sip of her wine, her demeanor and tone changing. "This isn't a friendly interview at all. I'm a murder suspect."

"No, not at all," Jason said. "We just need to be as thorough as possible."

Marcus squirmed.

Bernstein reached into her purse and took out what looked like a small calendar. She rifled through the pages.

"After Chuck's panel, I met with Sabrina Cook, a UCSD graduate student with an interest in my specialty. Marcus, you probably know her."

Marcus did and nodded.

"She asked me to be on her dissertation committee. Then I went back to my room, changed clothes, and took a taxi to the airport. I took Southwest flight 503 home to San Francisco at 5:30 p.m."

Jason was scribbling notes. "Thank you."

"Not at all. Is there anything else?" she asked, ice in her voice.

"No. Thank you for meeting with us."

And with that, Bernstein stood up, picked up her glass of wine, and threw it in Marcus's face.

25

Marcus wiped away what he could with a napkin. Jason tried hard not to laugh.

"Well," Marcus said, "at least we know she has a temper." He kept wiping.

"Yes. Also an alibi. I'll check it out, of course, but she didn't do it."

"I'm going home," Marcus said. "I may speak to you again at some point, but not for at least two years."

"Oh, come on."

"Okay, one year."

"Well, it will have to be sooner than that. Don't forget, we're flying to Chicago next week to talk to that University of Chicago guy."

Marcus groaned. What with Bob's accident and everything else, he had forgotten.

"Can't we interview him over the phone or something?"

"No. Cardinal rule. Always interview in person. Demeanor, expression, those things matter. And being there in person applies pressure to the witness."

"Do I have to go?"

"Yes. Come on, it's your home town. Don't you want a free trip? Show me the local flora and fauna?"

"It's January. In the Midwest, there's this thing called winter. It will be freezing. The wind will be howling off the lake. There will be two feet of snow. Or more."

Jason gave him a skeptical look as they got up and left. Everyone stared at Marcus's wet face and clothes.

When he got home, Cathy and Lily were both doing homework at the kitchen table.

"You smell like a derelict," Cathy said. "What happened?"

"Don't ask."

Lily laughed; Zelda came up and sniffed him, then walked away, a first.

He took a shower and began to relax. Later he told Bob what had happened, and Bob couldn't stop laughing.

Bob spent most of the weekend at the office, working with Anna, he said, on a upcoming case—a big, important one. Hopefully lucrative, too. Marcus had papers to grade. It was a quiet, peaceful weekend, which Marcus desperately needed. On Saturday evening, after Bob made lasagna, they played Monopoly with Lily, who won.

"She really is a whiz kid," Bob said. "Maybe we should talk to that school."

He meant the school for gifted children, the Mission Academy. Marcus nodded.

Bob dropped Marcus and Jason off at the airport on Monday morning for their trip, and, sure enough, it was 3 degrees when they landed in Chicago, huge piles of snow on the ground and icicles hanging everywhere. They took a cab to their hotel in the Loop and went to an Italian restaurant for dinner. They were set to speak to Liam Fraser at the University of Chicago the next morning.

"I can't believe this is the same planet," Jason said, shivering, "let alone the same country." Jason had spent his whole life in Southern California. He was wearing only a cotton sweater.

"I warned you," Marcus said, gloating.

After dinner Jason wanted to go to a gay bar, so Marcus gave him directions to one he remembered, hoping it was still there. Marcus wanted nothing more than to take a hot shower and fall asleep under a pile of blankets.

When he got out of the shower Jason had come back to the room.

"What happened?" Marcus asked.

"The place was deserted," Jason said, shrugging. They went to sleep in twin beds.

Marcus didn't sleep well; being back in Chicago always unsettled him. The city held very little for him except memories, most of them tinged with sadness.

He'd had a lonely, difficult childhood, which, he knew, was typical for gay men of his age. And he had a distant relationship with everyone in his family after coming out. His parents were now dead and his sister, the only relative who seemed to care about him at all, had moved to Denver when her husband landed a great job there. His few friends from high school had scattered all over the country. One or two gay friends had died early in the AIDS crisis.

Snow and sadness, that's what Chicago meant to him.

In the morning they had breakfast in the room, Jason wrapped in a blanket. Then they took a cab to the University on the south side.

The University of Chicago had opened in the late nineteenth

century, funded by Baptists, John D. Rockefeller, and Marshall Field
of the famous department store. It had a lovely central campus but
was surrounded on two sides by now-derelict neighborhoods. Even
now, after various waves of urban renewal, danger lurked just a few
blocks from campus, and student and faculty safety was a constant
issue. Still, the university was a powerhouse in the academic world,
full of brilliant scholars. A one-of-a-kind institution, one that
still took undergraduate teaching seriously while also excelling
at graduate education and research. Only Johns Hopkins and
Princeton came close, Marcus thought.

They met Liam Fraser in his office in one of the newer campus
buildings. He was a distinguished-looking man of about fifty,
dressed in a heavy, three-piece woolen suit. He suggested coffee, and
the three of them walked down the hall to a small kitchen, grateful
to have something hot to drink. As they served themselves, Fraser
asked, "So, gentlemen, what brings you all this way in January?"

Jason explained.

"Yes, it's true. We did not like each other. We disagreed
violently. But if you're thinking I had anything to do with his
murder, I'm afraid you came a long way for nothing."

Fraser explained that immediately after Chuck's session at
the MLA he had left for the airport. He showed them a receipt
from a cab company and his airline ticket, and his bill from his
convention hotel, which showed that he checked out right after
the session. Quickly computing the various times listed on the
receipts, Jason realized that Fraser couldn't possibly have followed
Chuck to La Jolla.

"Can you think of anyone who might have done this?" Jason
asked, hoping Fraser might have information that would mean
the trip hadn't been a total waste of time.

"Well, to be honest," he said, looking at Marcus, "I think you
should look closer to home."

"Meaning?" Marcus asked.

"Chuck and Margaret Garner were involved at one point. Then he dumped her."

26

Jason and Marcus looked at each other and tried not to look too shocked.

"How do you know this?" Jason asked.

"Well, they traveled together a bit, and I ran into them. In Amsterdam, after a conference. They were quite open."

"When was this?"

"I'm not quite sure. Wait."

Fraser got up and opened a file cabinet and rummaged through some folders, then did the same thing with the drawer below. He found what he was looking for.

"Yes, I remember now. It was five years ago. Here's the paper I delivered."

He handed the paper to Marcus; it had a date on it and the title "The Semiotics of Place."

"And you're sure they were together, and not just two colleagues at the same conference? Or who found themselves in the same city?"

"Quite sure. They stayed at the same hotel and were clearly involved. Hands all over each other. No question."

"And how do you know Professor Silver ended the affair?" Jason asked.

"He told me. The next time I saw him. Which was a few months later. In London."

"I see. What exactly did he say in London?"

"Well, he said Garner was upset. And that she threatened him in various ways. And then he said that he knew she really couldn't do anything without jeopardizing her own position, so he wasn't worried. He was quite nonchalant about the whole business."

"And do you know how long they were involved?"

"No, not really. My impression was, a few months, possibly a year. I've heard that was Silver's pattern. But I'm guessing."

Jason cleared his throat. "Well, thank you for that information, and for seeing us."

"Not at all. Sorry you had to come all this way for nothing. Have a good trip home."

In the cab back to the hotel, Jason asked Marcus if he believed the story about Maggie.

He thought for a moment. "I have no reason not to."

Jason pondered and then asked, "Would she have gone so far as murder? Or to pay for a hit?"

Marcus shrugged. He really didn't know what to say.

"I guess," Jason mused, "it might explain why she wanted you to talk to Emma, call off the investigation."

"Yes."

They checked out of the hotel and took the subway to O'Hare. Marcus slept on the plane while Jason fidgeted and read magazines.

They were both grateful to land in San Diego, where the temperature was 65 degrees and the sun was shining. They took separate cabs home after Jason said he would call Garner and set up an interview.

"You do that one alone," Marcus said. "I'm steering clear of her."

Jason agreed.

Two days later, Jason came over after dinner and recounted his meeting with Maggie Garner. Lily was doing homework in her room.

"That is one tough woman," he said over coffee.

"No kidding," Marcus said.

"She admitted the affair. It went on, she said, for about nine months. They did go to Amsterdam together, where they ran into Fraser. She said the affair was quite casual and they parted amicably."

"That's not what Fraser said," Marcus pointed out.

"No. And I'm not sure I believed her. But we really have no way of checking."

"Go on."

"I did ask her to account for her whereabouts on the day Silver died, and she said she and her husband were out of town, visiting family in San Francisco for the holidays. She showed me travel records."

"Of course," Bob said, "she could have hired someone to do the deed."

"Yes," Jason said. "I told her I would need access to her bank records, and she balked at that. She said she would not turn them over without a court order."

"Which you won't get, unless you can convince the cops or the DA that she's a real suspect," Bob said.

"Right."

"So, checkmate?" Marcus asked.

"I don't know. I'll talk to Sanchez, one of the detectives on the case. See how he reacts. But Marcus, you know her. Do you think she's capable of hiring someone to murder Silver? Now? The affair ended years ago."

"No, it doesn't make a lot of sense. I mean, she's tough. She's had to be, to get where she is. But to carry a grudge that long. I doubt it."

"So do I," Bob interjected from the dining room doorway. "Of course I don't know her, or the victim. But it doesn't sound to me like she's a real suspect."

Jason sighed. "We are getting nowhere, fast."

Marcus hesitated. "What about Julie Klein? Did her alibi check out?"

Jason nodded. "Yes. And the police checked her out. She's left-handed. The shooter wasn't."

"Ah," Marcus sighed. As much as he wanted to find Chuck's killer, he was relieved it wasn't Julie. Then he had a thought.

"Do you think you ought to ask Emma about Garner?" he asked. "I mean, it's tricky, Emma is still on the faculty. But maybe she knew about the affair. Or knows something one way or the other that would rule Garner in or out as a suspect."

"Yeah. Let me think about that."

Bob returned from the kitchen with more coffee and offered it around.

"Thanks, I've got to meet someone," Jason said.

"What's this one's name?" Bob asked, smiling.

"Mark," Jason said, smiling. "All gay men are named Mark, Rick, or Steve. And all gay men have track lighting," he said, imitating a Southern accent.

"Well, we don't," Bob said. "Track lighting is so twentieth century. And that's a line from a movie. And your Olympia Dukakis imitation is awful."

Lily came out and hugged Jason good-bye. He held onto her for a few seconds.

27

A few days later Jason and Marcus met Ed Peterson for lunch at a quiet restaurant in La Jolla. Peterson was not happy to be there; he made that clear from the moment he sat down.

"I know Chuck and I fought. We fought a lot. We were rivals. But to suspect me of murder is ridiculous. Why can't Emma just let the police do their work?"

That seemed to be the campus party line, Marcus told himself.

"We understand this is not pleasant," Jason said. "But the case against Isaacson is quite weak. Totally circumstantial. The police don't even have the murder weapon. So we need to ask you your whereabouts on the day Silver died. Just to be thorough."

Their conversation was interrupted by the arrival of their food.

"I was in Hawaii with my family. Staying at the Royal Westin on Maui."

"When did you leave, when did you get back?" Jason asked.

"We left on Tuesday of that week. Got back on the thirtieth. I'm sure the hotel has records. And I can show you the hotel bill."

"Right," Jason said, adding meekly, "I see. Well thank you."

"I'll be going now. That is, unless you're planning to detain me." He stood up and stormed off without touching his food.

Marcus gave Jason a dirty look.

"We had to ask," Jason said.

"I know, but this is getting ridiculous."

Jason nodded.

For a while they ate in silence, Marcus toying with a salad while Jason savored his club sandwich.

"You pay," Marcus said as he drained his coffee cup. "I'm going to the bathroom." All he wanted was to go back to his office, do some work, and forget about Chuck Silver.

Marcus had to pass through another dining area on his way to the bathroom. It was there that he saw them.

Bob was having lunch with Derrick something-or-other from the Stewarts' New Year's Eve party. The economist from Stanford by way of Harvard. The snob. Bob's back was facing Marcus, but he could see the side of his face.

And they looked exactly like two people who were in an intimate relationship.

28

Marcus felt very calm, the kind of calm that came over him at moments of true danger. The kind of calm that scared him. He forgot all about the bathroom and went back to join Jason.

"What's the matter?" Jason asked. "You're white as a sheet."

"What? Oh. Must have been something bad in the salad."

They got up, left the restaurant, and got into their cars. Jason said something about next steps, but Marcus wasn't paying attention.

He turned the ignition and lowered the windows, then turned off the engine. He sat for a long time. He felt dizzy, light-headed.

Finally, after a while, he looked at his watch and realized he needed to get back to campus to teach his class.

Later, he remembered nothing about that afternoon, driving to campus, teaching his class, office hours, driving home.

He did remember that when he got home, Cathy and Lily were playing in the back yard and Zelda greeted him, as usual, as if he had been away for months. It was a lovely, sunny day. He thanked Cathy, who left, and watched as Lily went to her room to do homework. Zelda followed her.

Marcus poured himself a glass of white wine and sat at the dining room table. He sat for a long time.

29

Around 6:00, Bob called and said he would be working late. Marcus pulled together a dinner of left-overs; as they ate, he asked Lily how school had been. She talked for a long time.

He didn't hear her, but smiled. He did the dishes and then suggested they take Zelda for a walk, thinking the exercise would clear his head.

It didn't.

When they got home, they watched TV for a bit, some cop show, and then Marcus tucked Lily into bed. He poured himself another glass of white wine and sat again at the dining room table.

Bob came in around 10:30.

"So," Marcus said, looking up. "Are you fucking him, or just thinking about it?"

30

B ob froze and turned bright red.

"I see," Marcus said.

"How did. . ."

"How did I find out? I was at the restaurant this afternoon. With Jason. I saw you together. On my way to the men's room."

"Oh."

"Yes, oh."

Bob started to cry.

Marcus had his answer.

31

M arcus slept, or tried to, in the extra bed in his study. In the morning, for Lily's sake, they did their best to act as if nothing had happened, and somehow made their way through it.

After Lily left for school—a friend's mother was picking her up—Marcus went into the bedroom to shower and change. He was on automatic pilot. Bob was already dressed and waited for him in the living room.

Marcus still felt that eerie kind of calm.

"I don't know what to say," Bob said, almost whispering

"When did it start?" Marcus asked.

"When you were in Chicago."

"And do you love him?"

"God, no. I love you. You know that."

"Do I?"

"Pinky. You know I do."

They sometimes called each other "Pinky," like Spencer Tracy and Katherine Hepburn in *Adam's Rib*, although neither had used the endearment in a long time.

"So it was what? Didn't mean anything. Is that what you want me to believe?"

"I was feeling lonely. I know that sounds crazy."

"You're right. It sounds crazy. I was gone for one night!"

"It's not just when you were away. I can't explain it. I guess . . ."

"You guess what?" He was getting angry for the first time since the restaurant.

"I don't know." Bob got up and looked out the front window. "It's just all been getting to me. Work. Dad. The accident, that night in the hospital."

"And the drinking," Marcus added.

"Yes. I've been drinking too much. You're right." Bob looked down, at his shoes.

Marcus gathered his things, his briefcase, keys, jacket.

"Okay, so here's what we're going to do. We're going to pretend things are normal, for Lily's sake. You're going to find a therapist. This week. Even if you have to postpone a case. Somehow we're going to get through the birthday party next week. Then we'll see."

Bob nodded. Marcus went to the front door. Opened it.

"And you are not going to touch another drop of alcohol."

Bob started to say something, then stopped himself. He nodded.

Marcus left. When he got into the car, he noticed that his hands were trembling.

32

They stumbled through the next few days, keeping their distance except when Lily was home, when they both did a fair job of acting normal.

"What's wrong, Pop?" Lily asked at one point. They never really could hide things from her for very long. She always knew when something was up.

"Oh, it's nothing sweet pea," he replied, smiling. "Just worried about a case at work."

They even slept in the same bed, turned away from each other, not wanting Lily to be suspicious. When they were alone, Bob said he had found a therapist and hadn't touched a drop of alcohol.

Marcus said nothing, but nodded.

Zelda, though, sensed something was wrong. Later, they both remembered her acting subdued as she went from one to the other, back and forth, back and forth.

On Sunday, Bob told Lily that he was going to the office, but whispered to Marcus that he was going to drive up to Laguna Beach to see Ruth. Marcus said he thought that was a good idea.

Bob found the drive calming. There wasn't much traffic, and the bright winter sun seemed to make everything sparkle, especially when the freeway passed close to the ocean. He especially noticed the graceful low mountains near Oceanside and Camp Pendleton, which, he knew, was the home of most of Jason's marines. That made him smile.

When he got to her house, Ruth hugged him, though she

could immediately tell something was wrong.

"What is it? Is Marcus okay? Lily?"

Bob teared up. "Lily is fine. But I've hurt him."

Ruth instantly switched into mother mode. "Come into the kitchen." Bob couldn't help but smile; at every crisis point in his life, that's exactly what his mother would say, ever since he was a little boy.

She made a pot of tea while Bob sat. After she poured the tea into two cups, she sat down and waited. Bob smiled again; he remembered the tea pot, the cups.

"So . . ." Ruth said.

"I cheated on him. I didn't mean to or plan it. It just happened."

Ruth closed her eyes, then opened them. She put her hand on top of his and nodded.

"I've gone into therapy. And stopped drinking, completely."

"Good."

"You were right about that. It started . . . it started getting bad when Dad died."

"I figured."

"And I'm turning forty. And Marcus and I have been together a long time."

"Yes, you have. But you still love him, don't you?"

"Yes. Absolutely."

"Are you sure?"

"Yes."

"Then it's simple. Not easy, but simple. You need to fix this. These things happen. In the best of marriages."

"Is that what we are, married? I guess we are."

"It happened to Alex and Carol."

"What? When?" Bob was truly shocked.

"When Carol was pregnant the second time. I was going

through cancer. Everything was a mess, remember, you all were flying back and forth across the country."

"I didn't know." Bob couldn't quite believe what he was hearing.

"No one did, not even your father. Carol confided in me." Ruth poured more tea.

Bob shook his head.

"Look," Ruth went on. "You made a mistake. A big one. So you make amends. And Marcus will forgive you, if you give him a chance. It could take a while, but I know he will. And don't forget . . ."

Bob finished her sentence. "We have a child."

"Yes. Exactly."

"I really messed up."

"Bobby, human beings mess up. Especially middle-aged men."

He laughed. "I guess that's what I am now. Middle-aged."

"It's not the end of the world, you know."

"No. I guess not."

And you do know, don't you," Ruth said, speaking very slowly, "that he's the best thing that ever happened to you?"

For the first time in a long time, all the noise in Bob's head stopped. He teared up.

Ruth smiled, got up and started making sandwiches for lunch. Bob got up and carried his cup of tea out to the balcony overlooking the ocean.

He inhaled, exhaled, and then listened to the waves.

33

Marcus graded papers in the morning. Lily left for a play date with a friend, and, on impulse, Marcus called Jason and suggested they have lunch.

They met at La Vache and Marcus asked for a quiet table in the back.

"What's up?" Jason asked, after they ordered.

"Bob had a fling with someone else."

Jason was stunned. He sat back in his chair.

"That day at the restaurant in La Jolla? When I got up to go to the bathroom? I saw them in the other room. Remember, you said I looked awful when I got back to the table."

"Right. Who is it?"

"Another faculty member. Someone new. They met at a New Year's Eve party. Blond, young, gorgeous. Your basic nightmare."

"That's a line from a movie."

Marcus laughed. "I know."

"Is it serious?" Jason asked.

"No, I don't think so. But . . ."

"Yeah. But." Jason shook his head.

Marcus tried to smile.

"You guys have been together a long time. I mean, a little short of twenty years, right?"

"Yeah. We met the year Bob finished college. He was 22. Now he's turning 40."

"You know, those guys who study gay couples, what's their names? You know the guys I mean. They live here, two shrinks. One of them is Mc-something."

"Right, I can't think of their names. I know who you mean."

"They say something like nine out of ten gay couples are not monogamous."

"I suppose that should make me feel better."

"No. Maybe. I mean . . . well I don't know what I mean." Jason looked away.

"He's gone into therapy. And stopped drinking. He says not

a drop."

"That's good. Very good. Look, you'll get through this. You have to. For Lily. And for both of you. I mean, you guys are the strongest couple I know."

"Were."

Jason scoffed. Marcus dug into his duck salad.

"By the way, I talked to Emma," Jason said after a while. "She wants to see us both."

"Oh, God. Why?"

"She's been going through Chuck's desk, his papers. She says she's found some things that might help the investigation."

Marcus sighed. "Okay. Maybe I need distraction, so I won't be able to think about my life falling apart."

"It hasn't fallen apart. You've hit a bump."

"A bump named Derrick. I should have known if it would happen in California, it would be with a gorgeous blond." Marcus rummaged his hand through his black-with-a-bit-of-gray hair.

"Derrick, Shmerick. It could have been Dave or Ron or Mike or Jeff. He doesn't matter. Not to Bob. I'm sure of it."

Marcus tried to smile and ate more of his salad.

34

On Monday, Jason called Marcus at his office, told him they were meeting Emma at 4:30. Then he called Bob at his office.

"We're having lunch," Jason told Bob.

"I can't today, too much work. Maybe later in the week."

"You're meeting me at 12:30 at the Crest, or I'm going to beat the crap out of you."

Bob paused for a moment. "Um. Okay. See you at the Crest."

He showed up on time, full of dread, knowing what was

coming. They both ordered turkey burgers.

"Okay, let me have it."

"Are you out of your fucking mind?"

"So he told you?"

"Yeah, he told me. Yesterday. You are such a cliché. Turn forty, cheat on your spouse. I mean, come on. At least be a little original. Dye your hair purple. Take up scuba diving. Change careers. But cheat on one of the best guys is California? Throw your life away? Do you know how lucky you are? You are out of your mind."

Bob opened his mouth to speak, but really didn't know what to say.

"In case you've forgotten, you have a child."

Bob looked down. "I know. Look, I didn't plan it. I feel awful. And I wish I could undo it. But I can't."

"Then get your head straightened out and then get down on your knees and beg him to forgive you."

Bob smiled a half-smile. "Okay."

They were quiet for a while. Their food came, and they ate mostly in silence.

On the sidewalk, Jason took Bob's arm and squeezed it hard. "I mean it. I was a cop, you know. I could beat the crap out of you and not leave an incriminating mark."

"Okay. I get it. Really. The great thing about you, Jason, is that you're straightforward."

"Damn right." He smiled his best Tab Hunter Hollywood smile. "Now fix this."

35

Marcus and Jason met Emma at her house later that afternoon, as arranged. Emma looked like her old self,

Marcus thought; in a word, lovely. She was wearing a cream-colored pant suit with a colorful blouse and high heels. He couldn't be sure, but it appeared she had lightened her hair a shade or two. Or perhaps it was just the late afternoon light streaming in. The light hit a painting that Marcus hadn't noticed before; it looked like it might be an original Miro.

She ushered them into the living room, offered tea or sherry; Marcus took a cup of tea. Emma asked how the investigation was going.

"Not too well, I'm afraid," Jason said. He then explained that so far, every suspect had an alibi. He detailed their encounters with Sandra Bernstein, Ed Peterson, and the trip to Chicago. Emma seemed quite amused by the wine-in-the-face part of the Bernstein story.

"Oh, Marcus. I'm sorry."

Marcus shrugged and smiled. He had all but forgotten the incident; in fact, he couldn't remember much about the previous few weeks, except the snow in Chicago. That stuck in his head.

"Well, this might help," Emma said. "I've been going through Charles's office, the one he kept here at home. It turns out he kept a sort-of journal. I never knew."

Jason suddenly sat up straighter, and Marcus paused the teacup as it was about to reach his lips.

Emma got up and retrieved a set of spiral notebooks from a table at the back of the room. They were ordinary, cheap notebooks, the kind students might use to take notes, one per class. She handed them to Jason. They had colorful covers, blue, red, green, yellow.

"His handwriting was atrocious, it always has been, and he used all sorts of abbreviations, initials to stand for various people, that sort of thing. But there's information there that should be useful."

"Right," Jason said. He tried not to appear too excited, but something like this was often the break in a case that investigators hoped for.

"Was there anything that jumped out at you?"

"Well, I haven't read them cover to cover, but yes. First, I don't think Fred Isaacson killed Charles. They were frenemies, if I can use that word. I never thought he was guilty, but now I'm sure."

"I see. We'll take a look, but you do have an obligation to turn these over to the police. Isaacson is facing a murder charge. These notebooks are evidence."

"I assumed as much, and I'll leave that to you. I assume you can make copies and then turn over whatever needs to be turned over."

Jason nodded.

"Anything else?"

"Well, yes. I always suspected that Charles had an affair with Maggie Garner. It didn't go on for very long, but it's clear Maggie didn't want it to end. She stalked Charles for a while. If that's the right word."

"I see."

"He also mentions some other people, people you would probably want to speak to. Other women." Emma looked down. It was clear Emma was choosing her words carefully. "Marcus might recognize the names, people in our field. Again, Charles used abbreviations, but I did recognize one or two names. And reading these, it became clear how Charles conducted these . . . adventures." Emma put as much sarcasm into that word as she could.

"And that was . . . ?" Jason prompted.

"He never saw anyone for very long, and then he would cut things off. And the women were often upset and pursued him. Like Maggie Garner."

"Are there dates on the entries?" Marcus asked.

"Yes, most of them. Not all."

"Well," Jason said, "thank you. This may be the break in the case we've been hoping for."

"I hope so." Emma got up and saw them to the door.

36

"Wow," Jason said as they walked to their cars.

"So what happens now?" Marcus asked.

"I'll have copies of everything made right away. We have to get the originals to the police quickly. They will be pissed off that she gave them to us first, and I don't want to risk an obstruction charge."

Marcus nodded.

"Then we go through them."

Marcus nodded again.

"Would you recognize Silver's handwriting? Take a quick look."

Over the years they had been colleagues, Marcus had received a few hand-written notes from Chuck.

"Yes, this looks like his writing."

"We'll have an expert confirm."

Marcus nodded again.

"What's your schedule like for the next week or so?" Jason asked.

Marcus told him. Classes, meetings, and Bob's party.

"Right, the birthday party."

Marcus winced.

"I'll have copies made immediately. Can you come over later tonight? We can start going through them."

Marcus was tired and couldn't think of anything he'd rather

do less than read a dead man's diary, but said yes, he was free. In fact, he would welcome a chance to get out of the house.

"Okay. Come over around 8:00."

Marcus drove home. Bob was cooking chicken piccata, and unsurprisingly, it smelled great. Bob was coming home on time these days and cooking, something he did really well.

"I have to meet Jason later," Marcus told him. "Can you stay with Lily tonight?"

"Yes of course. Is it a break in the case?"

"Maybe."

"That's good." Bob smiled. They had reached something of a thaw, where they were able to hold normal-sounding conversations.

Lily came in to the kitchen, followed by Zelda. They both greeted Marcus, Lily with a hug.

"How was school today?" Marcus asked, smiling.

"Boring," Lily said. She seemed unusually subdued.

"Honey, are those boys bothering you again?"

Some older boys had been making fun of Lily for having two fathers; when it started it had really upset her. Bob and Marcus had gone to the principal to complain, who said there was little she could do beyond talking to the boys, which they found pathetic. It was one of the reasons they were thinking of a new school.

"Um, a little," Lily said. "It's okay. I understand. They're just jerks."

Marcus and Bob glanced at each other, and both knew what the other was thinking; time to move her to the Academy.

Marcus fed Zelda and then they ate dinner, did a decent job of making small talk—Lily was excited about the upcoming party— and Marcus drove over to Jason's house just before 8:00.

Jason had two of the notebooks on the dining room table.

"Where are the rest?" Marcus asked.

"Still being copied. Hannah's doing it; she'll bring them when they're done." Jason shared his part-time assistant, and an office, with a bail bondsman named Barney.

"I've been going through them. These cover the last couple of years. He went for long periods without recording anything, then he'd go back to them for a while."

"And?"

"Well, Emma is right, Silver's feelings about Isaacson were more-or-less positive. He saw him as a rival, not really an enemy. But of course that doesn't tell us what Isaacson thought. But they did have lunch a lot, meet for drinks."

"So these don't exonerate him?"

"No, I wouldn't say so. Although they could be useful to his defense."

"What else?

"Some women. Look at this."

Jason showed him some passages from the previous spring about "EJ" in "AA."

Any idea who that is?

Marcus thought for a moment. "Eve Jacobs. She's a professor at Michigan. Ann Arbor."

"Ah! Ann Arbor. I was thinking, you know, AA for drunks."

Marcus laughed.

There were a few passages about Jacobs, and Emma was right, it was clear she didn't want the affair to end. In one passage Chuck had written "I wish to God she'd stop calling."

Jason showed him another set of passages. "Who could this be?" The passages referred to "JennL" in "UWS."

"That's Jennifer Lindsey. She teaches at Columbia. 'UWS' is the Upper West Side."

"Right. New York." For a native Californian like Jason, Manhattan might as well be Mars. That was the thing about

California, Marcus had learned; the rest of the country, especially the Midwest and the East coast, were far, far away. Marcus saw that attitude in his many of his students, almost all natives, at least the undergraduates. Oh, DC. Oh, Congress. All that stuff, back East.

Chuck's passages about Lindsey had the same tone as those about Eve Jacobs; some amorous encounters, then a cooling off and Lindsey wanting things to continue.

"How did this guy do it?" Jason asked. "I mean, he was middle-aged, and he wasn't exactly a male model. Why were so many women attracted to him?"

Marcus thought for a moment. "Intellect. Fame. Culture."

Jason let that sink in.

Marcus looked through some other passages. What stood out to him was tenderness toward Emma and Chloe. There was no question but that Chuck loved his family, loved them deeply. When he wrote about them he detailed everything, what they wore, what they said.

Marcus said as much to Jason.

"Yeah, clearly." And then Jason added a phrase that stuck with Marcus for a long time.

"And he liked fast food sex."

Marcus had wondered how Chuck managed to keep both things going at the same time, a happy home life with a wife and child, and then his affairs, all carried on while teaching, writing, conferencing. It made Marcus tired just to think about it. Chuck must have had the energy of a twenty-year-old. Clearly, though, he needed, or wanted, both, both halves of his life.

"What about Maggie Garner?" Marcus asked.

"She must be in earlier notebooks, don't have those yet."

Marcus felt relieved; he knew Garner's involvement could lead to a scandal on campus if she became a real suspect in Chuck's murder, or even if word of the affair got out. He knew that Chuck would probably write about her, but he was glad for a temporary reprieve.

"So," Jason said. "We need to go East again. Ann Arbor and New York."

Marcus sighed. "After the party."

37

The next few days were taken up with the preparation for Bob's birthday party. Food and alcohol and rented china and crystal were delivered. Marcus had rented an extra refrigerator as well, which they put on the back patio, for all the food and to chill the champagne. Bob's nephew Jay came over the night before the party and helped put up the decorations, balloons and streamers. Lily was ecstatic. Jay stayed overnight, sleeping in Marcus's study. Together he and Marcus moved some of the furniture out of the living room and into Lily's playroom to make room for all the guests.

"Oh, God, I'm too old for this," Marcus said as they carried a heavy chair.

Lily was so excited the morning of the party she wanted to stay home from school, but they put their foot down. Reluctantly, she went. When Ruth arrived around noon, laden with cakes and cookies she had baked, she, like every mother in history, began wiping down the spotless kitchen sink. Both Bob and Marcus had taken the day off from work.

Alex and Carol arrived early, around 6:00, and they all ate a quick meal of tuna casserole Carol had brought. The guests began arriving at 8:00.

They had invited everyone they knew, people from the neighborhood, friends, faculty friends of Marcus's from campus, legal colleagues of Bob's, a judge or two, and even a few of his former clients.

"Really?" Marcus had said when he saw the guest list Bob had put together. "Wasn't this one charged with grand larceny?"

"We'll count the silver after he goes," Bob had joked.

That was before. Marcus realized as he dressed for the party that his life now had a before and an after.

The house filled up quickly and everyone was in a good mood. They had said "no gifts please" on the invitation but many brought things anyway, and they put them in a pile in the corner. Zelda greeted everyone with her madly wagging tail, going from person to person, demanding to be petted. She loved a crowd.

Both Marcus and Bob did their best to act normal. They put on music, some of their favorite records, Glenn Miller, Ella Fitzgerald singing Cole Porter, Sarah Vaughn, and, when it got late, the Supremes. A few people danced, including Jason and Anna, and everyone seemed to be having a good time. Marcus noticed that Bob drank only mineral water, not champagne.

To Marcus's surprise, both Emma Baker and Maggie Garner came, separately, both arriving late. Emma wore a black pant suit, and Maggie, a bright red dress and too much makeup. They managed to stay away from each other until Emma used the bathroom. When she came out, she came face to face with Maggie.

It was clear to Marcus from the expression on her face that she had dipped into Chuck's diary and found confirmation of his affair with Maggie. It was one thing to suspect it, Marcus thought, and another thing to see it spelled out, removing all doubt.

"Hello, Emma, how are you," Maggie said, in what Marcus knew to be her most insincere, haughty voice, the voice she used at meetings when she thought a faculty member's question was stupid.

"I'm fine, Maggie, thanks," she said, very slowly, picking up her glass of champagne where she had left it, on a bookshelf. Then she looked directly at Maggie. "Sleep with anyone else's husband lately?"

It was quite late and the crowd had thinned out. Several people heard the exchange and stopped chatting. Marcus heard it too and froze. For just a moment, the only sound in the room was Diana Ross.

Maggie turned bright red, went into the bedroom to retrieve her coat, and left without saying a word.

Emma, cool and calm, walked over to the dining room table and picked up one of the slices of cake arrayed on plates.

"Mmm, coconut. I love coconut," Emma said, smiling.

Rudd Martin, who had witnessed the scene with Maggie, came and stood next to Emma. "Yes," he said. "The cake is wonderful." He was, as usual, wearing a dramatic scarf, this time on top of a jet-black sweater and black slacks.

Chatter resumed. Bob, who had been in the kitchen, walked up to Marcus and asked him what had just happened; he had caught the end of the scene.

"A little faculty warfare. I'll tell you later." Marcus swallowed a large gulp of champagne.

Another faculty member came up to Marcus. "Well. That was like the party scene in *All About Eve*."

Marcus and Bob both laughed. "Yes, I know," Marcus replied. "And where is Celeste Holm when you need her?"

Finally, about midnight, everyone was gone except family; they collapsed around the living room. Jay was spread out on the floor in the shape of a cross, with Zelda resting her head on his chest. Lily wanted to stay up but Bob said it was way past her bedtime.

"Okay, okay. Slavedriver." She hugged or kissed everyone good-night.

"If they're mean to you, sweetie, you come live with me,"

Ruth said, and Lily laughed and hugged her grandmother.

"Come on, Marcus," Carol said, "I'll help you in the kitchen."

Marcus groaned but followed her. They started loading the dishwasher.

"So," Carol said after a while, "I gather we're both married to less than perfect men." Bob had told Marcus about Alex, which, in some strange way, made Marcus feel slightly better. Maybe there was a gene for cheating.

For a moment Marcus stopped moving. He didn't know what to say. He was touched that Carol was confiding in him, but also incredibly embarrassed. He didn't know how to react.

"I guess so," he said after a long moment.

"It's hell, I know. But you do get beyond it."

"So you were able to forgive Alex?"

"Yes. After a while. I finally decided that what we had together mattered a lot more than a fling. And that's all it was. And I'm sure that's what it was for Bob. I mean, with Jake dying the way he did . . ." She didn't finish the sentence.

Marcus nodded.

"And it helped that Alex groveled."

Marcus laughed and Carol smiled.

"Marriage is hard," Carol said. "When it lasts. I know that probably sounds so Oprah. But it can't all be hearts and flowers. A man is a man is a man. Gay or straight. You know, someone with a penis."

They both laughed.

"I guess so. The thing is . . ." Marcus hesitated.

"What?"

"I've never had the urge."

"You're wired differently. But I'd bet you're the rare exception. In fact, I'm sure of it."

"Maybe so." Marcus hadn't thought about it in those terms.

"Don't forget . . ."

"I know. Lily."

Carol nodded. She turned to retrieve some plates on the kitchen table, and stopped.

She saw Jay standing in the doorway, holding some glasses. The look on his face made her blood run cold.

38

Jay put down the glasses. He turned around and went to Marcus's study, where he had slept, and slammed the door.

Alex came into the kitchen. "What just happened?"

"We were talking, and he must have overheard us. We didn't know he was there." Carol was feeling rising panic.

It took a moment for Alex to grasp what his wife meant.

"Oh, Jesus. We agreed . . ."

"Well, I didn't do it on purpose," Carol said. "It was an accident."

Alex shook his head. "One of us needs to go talk to him."

"Not tonight," Carol said. "Let him sleep. We'll come back early in the morning." They, and Ruth, were staying at a local hotel.

Alex nodded, looking really upset. Bob followed Jay from the living room and knocked on the door.

"Jay, are you all right?" he called.

Jay came out of the bedroom wearing his jacket. He gave Bob a dirty look, and then gave his father, now in the living room, a look that terrified him.

"I'm going for a walk. I need clean air," he said, looking at his father, who turned bright red.

Jay was out the front door before anyone could say anything.

"He shouldn't be walking around alone at this hour," Ruth said.

"He'll be okay," Alex said. "We should let him be. He's had a shock."

Ruth put two and two together and took a long, deep breath.

Carol and Marcus finished cleaning up what they could in the kitchen, and everyone sat in the living room. It was now after 1:00 a.m.

"You guys go back to the hotel," Marcus said. "I'll go look for him."

"I'll go with you," Bob said.

"No. You go to sleep. I'll go," Marcus said.

"That's best," Carol said. "We'll come over early in the morning."

Bob nodded. Alex and Carol and Ruth gathered their things, and, after a round of hugs, drove back to their hotel.

Marcus got in his car, sighed, and drove around the neighborhood. He found Jay sitting on a bench in a small nearby park. Marcus got out and sat next to him. He waited for Jay to talk. It was a chilly night.

From many years of dealing with troubled students, he knew it was best to wait and let them speak.

"How could he? How could Bob?" Jay said, finally. He sounded more sad than angry, which, Marcus thought, was a good sign.

"Listen, it's not an excuse. Or even an explanation. But these things happen. Even to people who love each other. People do stupid things sometimes."

Jay scoffed.

"Come back to the house, get some sleep. Your parents will be here in the morning and you'll talk."

"No. I don't want to talk to him," Jay said.

"Jay, he's your father. He loves you. And he loves your mother."

"Take me back to campus."

"Now??"

"Yes, now. Please."

"Okay, if that's what you really want. But you know you'll have to talk to them about this, sooner or later."

"I know. But not right now."

Marcus nodded.

They stopped at the house and Jay picked up his overnight bag. Bob was in the shower.

They were both quiet on the drive to campus.

By the time Marcus got home, it was 2:45. Bob was still up, and Marcus filled him in.

"Oh, God," was all Bob said. They went to bed.

39

Lily and Zelda got up at their usual time, around 6:00, and both Bob and Marcus dragged themselves out of bed, completely exhausted.

"Where's Jay?" Lily asked over breakfast.

"Oh," Marcus said, "he had to get back to school."

"But it's Saturday," Lily said, confused.

"I know sweet pea," Bob said, "but he has a lot of homework. That happens in college. Don't you have some too?"

"Yeah," she said, dejectedly. "Boring math. It's way too easy."

"Why don't you do it now, get it out of the way?" Marcus suggested.

"Okay, okay." She went off to her room, and Zelda trotted along after her.

Around 8:00, Alex and Carol arrived, looking tired. They said Ruth was driving back to Laguna Beach. Wisely, Marcus thought.

"Where's Jay?" Alex asked.

Marcus told them what happened.

"Oh," was all Alex said. He looked like he had aged overnight.

"Listen," Marcus said. "Give him time. Call him in a few days, then arrange to see him. Together."

Carol said that made sense. Alex nodded, reluctantly.

They sat silent over coffee, and when they were finished, Alex and Bob moved the furniture back in place while Marcus and Carol took down the streamers from the party. Most of the balloons had fallen to the floor. They gathered up all the trash and stuffed it into plastic bags.

"We should get going, collect Ruthie," Carol said. They had let their daughter sleep over at a friend's house.

"Take some cake for her," Bob said, wrapping up a huge slice from the vast amount of leftovers.

"Alex," Marcus said, "I'm sorry for what happened with Jay last night. We just didn't see him standing there."

"I know," Alex said. He put his hand on Marcus's shoulder. "It's not your fault. It's mine."

Carol hugged them both at the front door, and they were off.

"Well," Bob said after they had gone, "between Emma and Maggie and Jay, that was a party for the ages."

Marcus laughed. "Emma and Maggie. God. I had almost forgotten. I'm supposed to go over to Jason's today, go through the rest of Chuck Silver's diaries."

They took turns in the shower, and then the phone rang. It was Jason, suggesting Marcus come over after lunch.

"Hell of a party," he said.

"Yeah. Tell me about it."

Both Bob and Marcus settled on the bed. Bob put his head on Marcus's shoulder, and Marcus stroked his hair.

40

After a light lunch of tomato basil soup, Lily's favorite, and tuna salad, Marcus drove over to Jason's house. Bob said he'd take Lily and Zelda to the park. When Zelda heard the word "park," she started dancing in circles.

"Well, you look like shit," Jason said as Marcus walked in.

"Why, thanks. That's just the look I was going for."

"Not much sleep?" Jason said hopefully.

"No, not much, but not for the reason your dirty mind is thinking."

"Oh."

Marcus looked around. "What, no soldier in a towel?"

"I'm thinking of joining the priesthood. So I'm practicing," Jason deadpanned.

"Ohhhhh."

"That was quite a scene between Emma and Maggie last night," Jason said, pouring Marcus a cup of coffee.

"I know. There must be stuff in the diaries. Emma must have looked through them."

"There is. A lot." Copies of the diaries were spread out on his kitchen table, with marks on some of the pages. He must have already turned over the originals to the police, Marcus thought, pulling some sheets over to his side of the kitchen table. He started to read.

"What's interesting about last night," Jason said, "is that maybe Emma wasn't as okay with Chuck's screwing around as she led us to believe."

"Yeah, I thought of that. But Maggie could be a special case to Emma. I mean, she's the boss. Of both of them. Emma might have thought the affair would have an impact on her professional life. Or on Chuck's. Or both."

"Say more."

"Well," Marcus went on, "we go through these constant merit reviews at UCSD, and Maggie is the one who has the most important voice in that. It affects your salary, your standing on campus. It's an obnoxious system, but there's no escape. Plus that new research center. Maggie would have the final word on who ran it, how it was set up, all of that."

"Or," Jason said, thinking out loud, "Emma might have worried what people would think if word got out on campus about the affair. You're always saying there are no secrets in your world, and now that the police have the diaries . . ."

"Mmm, yes," Marcus said. He was absorbed in reading the passages Jason had marked.

Chuck described the affair with Maggie as "hot" and "volatile." He wrote about having sex on the couch in Maggie's office, which shocked him—there'd be so many people around in the outer offices-- and at the apartment in Pacific Beach. At one point he described Maggie as "insatiable" and "jealous." He mentioned the trip to Amsterdam. Looking at the dates, it seemed that the affair lasted about six or seven months, starting about five years before.

And, perhaps most interesting, was this.

Maggie told me today she wants to divorce George. I said nothing. And then she said she wanted me to divorce Emma, she wants to marry me. I told her she was dreaming, and she picked up a book and threw it at me.

A few weeks later, there was another entry, cryptic but explosive.

MG has started issuing threats.

"Wow," Marcus said, looking at Jason.

"Yeah. Motive."

"Except she was out of town at the time of the murder," Marcus said.

"Right, and that alibi checked out. But she could have paid

for a hit."

"How do we find out?"

"The cops have to. They'll need a court order for her bank records, her phone records, all of that. See if there's any evidence of hiring a hit man."

"Have you talked to them?"

"I talked to Sanchez when I gave him the originals of the diary. Didn't get a firm sense of what was happening."

"Don't they need to look into her as a suspect?"

"I don't know, I don't know who is really in charge of the investigation. I do know . . ."

"What?"

"They'll be reluctant to admit they arrested the wrong perp."

"Right."

Both of them were quiet for a moment.

"You know Maggie. Can you imagine her hiring a killer?" Jason asked.

Marcus stood up, poured more coffee, and leaned against the kitchen counter.

"I just don't know. She has a ruthless streak, no question. But would she jeopardize her whole life, her career over an affair? I mean, Maggie is relatively young for a senior administrator. She's in her early fifties, I think."

"Does she have kids?"

"A daughter at UCLA, I think."

"So, out of the house."

"Right. She's all about work at this point. Very ambitious. She'll probably be a university president somewhere within a few years. Would she risk throwing all that away?"

"Crazier things have happened. I mean, passion. It makes people crazy."

Marcus remembered the case of Jean Harris, the former

headmistress of an exclusive Virginia girls' school who was convicted of murdering her lover, a famous diet doctor. What Jason said made sense. But he still had a hard time believing a member of the academy could be a murderer. He said so.

"Almost anyone is capable of murder," Jason said.

"I know, Bob says the same thing. Do we interview Maggie again?"

"No, not yet. We let the police deal with it. For a while. But we talk to Emma again."

Marcus hated that idea, but nodded. "What else is in here?" he asked, pointing to the pages.

"More women, so more possible suspects. Does the name Karen Stein ring a bell?"

"Yes. She's in the philosophy department."

Jason pointed to some passages. Same pattern, hot sex for a while and then, nothing.

"And do the initials DG mean anything to you? This one is recent."

Marcus thought. "DG. DG. Not offhand. So . . . what's the next step?"

"Back to Emma. Talk to Stein. And plan that trip East."

Jason showed Marcus the passages about Eve Jacobs in Michigan and Jennifer Lindsey in New York. Yet again, hot and heavy for a period of months, then Chuck cutting things off.

And there were any number of tender, touching passages about Emma and Chloe.

"How did he do it? I mean, psychologically? Live these two separate lives?" Bob wondered out loud.

Jason shrugged. "Men."

41

In a few days, Jason called Marcus at his office to say he had met with Sargent Sanchez and that the police were following up with Maggie Garner as a suspect. They insisted Isaacson was the perp, but, in their words, "just to be thorough," they would get a subpoena for Maggie's bank and telephone records. She had then quickly hired Darren Jacobs as her attorney.

"He's a big gun," Jason said. "He's tough. Very tough. And the judges love him." Marcus knew the name; Bob had tangled with Jacobs in court, and had the same assessment.

Jason then asked Marcus to set up a meeting with Karen Stein.

Marcus knew Karen, although not terribly well; she was an expert on the philosopher Immanuel Kant and well-respected on campus and among philosophers. She was married to Marvin Stein, another member of the department, who had written books on Hegel and on Karl Marx. They had been friendly to Marcus and had even had Bob and Marcus to dinner soon after they arrived in San Diego, although they didn't see much of them after that. Marcus had invited them to dinner a few times, but they always said they were busy; after a while, he stopped asking. Still, he was reluctant to ask her to a meeting.

Karen suggested they meet her at home. Jason told her they needed to talk to her about personal matters and she might not want to have that conversation in front of her husband.

"No, it's fine," she said cryptically.

They met the following evening at 6:00 in the Steins' large house in Del Mar, north of the UCSD campus. It was one of those ultra-modern, concrete houses with windows in strange shapes that had been popular in the 1970s but now looked outdated and silly. Inside, though, it was lovely. The

Steins softened the concrete walls with warm, colored tapestries, bright paintings, and comfortable furniture. And there were books everywhere.

Marvin opened the door and ushered them into the den, where Karen was waiting. She got up, and Marcus introduced Jason. Marvin offered drinks, which they both declined; both he and Karen were drinking white wine. They were both around fifty with brown hair and strong, athletic-looking bodies. They had met in graduate school at Yale.

"So," Jason said, "I've been retained by Emma Baker to look into her husband's death, as I said on the phone. Emma does not believe Fred Isaacson committed the murder, and the case against him is quite weak."

"Yes," Marvin said. "We don't think Fred did this either. We know him quite well. He and Chuck fought a great deal, but nothing too out of the ordinary, at least on this campus. I mean, people are fighting over the spoils all the time. We're a growing campus, lots of money sloshing around."

Marcus nodded. What Marvin said was true.

"I need to ask you a question, Mrs. Stein, based on a diary Mr. Silver kept. I know this is highly personal."

"That's quite all right." She seemed completely calm.

"It appears from the diary that you and Mr. Silver were, for a time, intimate."

Karen Stein looked over at her husband and smiled.

"Yes, that's true."

"We are candid with each other," Marvin quickly added. "We don't keep secrets."

"I see," was all Jason could think of to say. "How did it start, and how did it end, if you don't mind my asking?"

"I don't mind at all. We met at a sex party," Karen said, in a completely relaxed voice without a hint of embarrassment.

Both Marcus and Jason did their best to hide their reaction.

"I was there as well, in case you were wondering," Marvin added.

"And where was this?"

"It was in Palm Springs, right around the first of the year . . . it must have been at the beginning of 2000. I remember because of *Bush vs. Gore*."

Marvin nodded.

"And you were intimate with Mr. Silver at this party?"

"Yes."

"And . . ."

"And we enjoyed each other, and continued to see each other, one-on-one."

"And who hosted this sex party?"

"That I'm not prepared to divulge," Karen said. "We've spoken to our attorney, once we knew you were going to be asking us these questions. He urged us to be candid about our own activity, but go no further."

"I see. Let me ask this. To your knowledge was Mr. Silver intimate with anyone else at that party?"

She seemed to be thinking. "Honestly, I don't remember," Karen said, turning to her husband.

"No, neither do I," Marvin added.

"And how long did your affair continue?" Jason asked.

"Six or seven months, on and off," Karen said, while Marvin refilled her wine glass.

"And where would you meet?"

"Chuck had an apartment down in Pacific Beach. We'd meet there. Or here."

"Did the affair end amicably?"

"Yes, completely. Chuck wasn't one for long-term commitments, except to Emma, of course. He made it completely clear he was devoted to Emma and was not interested in any involvement beyond the physical, although of course we talked."

"About?"

"Oh, current events, campus politics, the usual."

"I see. Is there anything you're aware of that might help us find who did this to Mr. Silver? Did he ever mention a feud with someone, or anything like that? Even a casual remark might be helpful."

Karen thought for a moment. "No. Nothing I can think of."

"Well," Jason said, "if you do think of anything, please give me a call." He handed her one of his business cards.

"Of course."

"Just for the record, where were both of you when Chuck died? That was Friday, December 27th."

"We were in London that week," Marvin said. "Staying at Claridge's. I'm sure they can verify."

"Thanks."

They all got up and Marvin walked them to the door. He turned to Marcus.

"I hope we haven't shocked you," Marvin said, good-naturedly.

Marcus smiled. "Only a little."

Back in Marcus's car, he turned to Jason. Marcus let out a deep breath.

"Quite a little hotbed, your campus," Jason said.

"Yeah. Who knew. I mean, do you really think they could be so completely blasé about all this?"

"Well," Jason said, "if they're not, they sure as hell are good actors."

42

A few days later, Karen Stein called Jason. "I did remember something that might be helpful," she said.

Jason was all ears.

"Chuck and I met for coffee recently. He mentioned someone who went by her initials, DG. I don't know who it was. But I got the impression they had been involved."

"I see. Do you recall exactly what he said?"

"No, I'm sorry, at this point I don't. But I do remember the conversation, and I'm sure I got the initials right. I remember because the letters rhymed."

"Did it seem like it was someone from your campus?"

"I don't know. It could be. It's a huge place. 16,000 students, thousands of faculty and staff."

"Of course. Anything else you remember?"

"Sorry, no."

"Well thank you for calling. And for being so candid the other evening."

"Not at all. Truth is always best."

Jason then arranged a meeting for late that afternoon with Emma and Marcus.

Marcus didn't want to go. He was feeling more and more uncomfortable being mixed up in an investigation that involved so many academic colleagues, not to mention a senior administrator. But Jason convinced him he really needed him to be there, and that Emma wanted him there as well.

"Why does she want me there?" Marcus asked. "It makes no sense."

"Someone from her world. And you did find Chuck's body."

"Yes, but . . ."

Jason cut him off. "I've seen this before, with survivors of murder victims. It's some kind of psychological thing. You're a link to the dead guy. I know it's irrational, but it happens."

"I see." Marcus said, though he didn't.

"And I need you. I'm completely lost in sorting through all this academic intrigue."

So Marcus agreed to see Emma that afternoon.

Jason was glad to keep Marcus busy with interviews. He didn't want his friend to brood over Bob's affair. He knew too many gay couples who broke up over affairs and lived to regret it.

They arranged to meet at Emma's house at 4:30, when Marcus was done with his day on campus. As he stood at his desk gathering up his things to leave, there was a knock on the door. It was Jay.

Marcus noticed that something was different about him. In the late afternoon light coming in from his western-facing window, he couldn't figure out what it was. New haircut? Different expression on his face?

"Hey," Jay said simply, when he walked in. He could see Marcus was about to leave. "Is this a bad time?" Marcus noticed his jeans were ripped at the knees.

"Hey. I have a meeting I have to get to, I'm afraid. It's not one I can miss. But how are you?"

"Well, better than I was the other night."

"Good. Can we meet tomorrow? Maybe for lunch?"

"Sure." They arranged it.

"I'm sorry I have to rush off." They walked out of the building together. As Marcus got into his car, he watched Jay walk away and he realized what was different. Somehow, Jay looked a bit older. In just a few days, he looked older.

43

Marcus drove to Emma and Chuck's house and found Jason waiting in his car. They knocked, and Rudd Martin opened the door.

"Ah, *les enquêteurs*. Bonjour."

Jason hadn't met Rudd and had no idea what he had just heard.

"Forgive me, Emma and I were conversing in French. That wasn't an insult, I promise."

Emma emerged from the kitchen, chuckling.

"It means 'the investigators.'" She introduced Rudd to Jason.

"I was just leaving, I was dropping off Emma's campus mail," Rudd said. "Take care, Emma." He kissed her chastely on the cheek.

As he left Chloe came running in and clasped her mother around her legs. Emma smiled and introduced Marcus and Jason. Chloe was lovely; she smiled her mother's smile and said hello. Marcus judged her to be perhaps seven or eight years old. She had large eyes and soft brown hair.

"Mummy, may I watch some television?"

"Yes, pet. But please keep the volume low."

Marcus noticed the word "may." Lily would have said "Can I." Chloe ran off, smiling.

Emma motioned for Jason and Marcus to sit, and a maid emerged.

"Can I get you anything? Tea? Coffee? A drink? Something to eat?"

They both shook their heads.

Emma nodded to the maid and she disappeared.

"So, where are we?" Emma asked, crossing her legs.

"We need some information about names mentioned in your husband's diaries," Jason said.

"Of course."

"Were you aware of an affair between Mr. Silver and Margaret Garner, roughly five years ago?"

Emma's expression changed from a slight smile to neutral. "At the time, I only had a suspicion."

"Forgive me, but I need to ask this."

"Please."

"Did that particular affair worry you, or concern you?"

"Yes, it did." Emma looked down at her nails.

"And why was that?"

Emma looked up. "Because Maggie was in charge of the campus." She looked over to Marcus.

"I've explained Maggie's position," Marcus said quickly.

"Then you can see the problem. Chuck's dalliances never lasted very long. I was worried that there would be hard feelings, and that Maggie could use her position to retaliate in some way."

"Against your husband, or against you?"

"Either, both."

"What kind of retaliation?"

"All sorts went through my mind. Our salaries could have suffered, for one thing. Fundraising for this new center Chuck was hoping to establish."

"I see. Was your concern one of the reasons the affair ended?"

"I imagine so, yes." She brushed her hair away from her ears.

"Your husband in his diary mentions 'threats' from Ms. Garner. Were you aware of those threats? Do you know any specifics?"

"I was aware that Maggie seemed to turn quite negative toward Charles at one point. Looking back, I'm not surprised if she made threats. But I don't know what they were."

"Were you aware that Maggie wanted to marry Mr. Silver?" Jason asked.

Marcus flinched and hoped it wasn't too obvious.

"Yes, he mentioned it. Neither one of us took it seriously."

"Even when threats were made?"

"Well as I say, I don't know what those threats were. But for one thing, such a marriage would have required two divorces. That would have been quite the campus scandal, even here in La Jolla among the lotus-eaters. I'm sure Marcus can attest to that."

"Yes, I agree. It would have caused a scandal. And that might have cost Maggie her position, and any future position," Marcus added.

"And," Emma added, "I knew Charles would never divorce me. Certainly not when Chloe was young."

She got up and poured herself a sherry. She motioned with the bottle toward both Marcus and Jason, and they both shook their heads.

Jason went on.

"I know this may seem far-fetched, but can you imagine Margaret Garner wanting your husband dead?"

Emma sat down, took a sip of sherry, and then looked up with an amused expression, which unsettled both Jason and Marcus. In fact, it gave Marcus chills.

"Yes."

Jason remained calm. "Please elaborate."

"About a year or so ago, Chuck started an affair with Maggie's daughter, Danielle."

It took a moment for that to sink in.

Jason cleared his throat. "Danielle Garner. DG in the diary."

"Yes."

"And do you know how her mother reacted?"

"Apparently she was livid. She confronted Charles about it at least twice that I know of. Charles told her Danielle was an adult and capable of making her own decisions, which was of course true."

"How long did the affair with Danielle last?"

"I couldn't say. We were back in our usual mode of not talking about these things."

"Have you told the police any of this?"

"They asked me about Maggie, and about DG, yesterday, in fact, and I told them what I've just told you."

"I see."

"Will they investigate?" Emma asked.

"Yes, they will have to, now."

"And does that mean they will let poor Fred Isaacson go?"

"That I couldn't say."

Emma nodded.

"Well," Jason said, "I think we have everything we need for today. Thank you for your time, and your candor."

Emma saw them to the door.

Out on the driveway, they both leaned against their cars.

"I feel," Jason said, "like we've stumbled into the academic version of Peyton Place."

"No," Marcus said. "Closer to Valley of the Dolls."

When Marcus got home, Bob was sitting at the kitchen table with Lily and Anna, playing gin. Something delicious-smelling was in the oven.

"Gin!" Lily cried.

"That's it, I'm never doing this again, you're too good," Anna said. Lily giggled.

"We've got some work to do, so I invited Anna to dinner. Then this gambler forced us to play cards," Bob said, reaching over and tickling Lily. She howled.

The casserole in the oven turned out to be turkey tetrazzini, which they ate with salad and homemade pecan cookies for dessert. After dinner, Lily had homework and Bob and Anna started working at the dining room table. Marcus went into his study and prepared his next class.

After Anna left and Lily was asleep, they sat on the living room sofa. Bob put his head in Marcus's lap.

44

The next day Marcus met Jay for lunch on campus at the faculty club. Jay always felt awkward in a setting with so many professors, but they both loved the salad bar and, especially, the club's bread, which tasted homemade. And parking was such a hassle on campus that it didn't pay to drive somewhere off campus for lunch.

"So," Marcus said after they fetched their food and sat down.

"So."

"Have you been home?"

"No, but I've been to Laguna."

"Oh?" Marcus asked with surprise.

"Yeah. Granny called and invited me for dinner. I borrowed my roommate's car and drove up."

"And?"

"Well, she mostly listened, and then she told me that what dad did happens in a lot of marriages. In fact . . ."

"What?"

"Well, she kinda hinted that it might have happened to her. I mean, that maybe granddad cheated on her once."

Marcus put down his fork. "Really?"

"Yeah. I was surprised too. Shocked. She didn't say too much about it. And she didn't come right out and say it. But she talked a lot about forgiveness."

"I'm really surprised. About your grandfather. Not surprised that she forgave him."

"Yeah, I was really surprised too. She said something interesting about men as they get older, that it can be hard to let go of that part of themselves, the wilder part, the part that's gotten domesticated."

"I suppose that could be true."

A colleague he hadn't seen for a while stopped at the table and Marcus shook his hand and they chatted for a minute.

"Sorry about that," Marcus said to Jay. "Do you think you can forgive your dad?"

"I'm working on it."

"You should talk to him. And to your mom."

"I will. I promise. What about you?"

"You mean, can I forgive your uncle?"

"Yeah."

"I'm working on it too."

"You've been together so long . . ."

"Yes. We have. That makes it . . ." Marcus hesitated, groping for words ". . . both harder to forgive and easier to understand what happened." Marcus was startled. He had never articulated it this way before, even to himself.

Jay seemed lost in thought. Eventually he looked at his watch and said he had to get to his bio lab.

"Bio lab?"

"I'm thinking pre-med. Maybe."

"Oh, my. Don't you kinda have to do pre-med from the moment you get here? Or start in high school?"

"Well, I've been doing that. Sort of. We'll see."

They left the club together and in front, they hugged.

On his way back to his office, and on the drive home later, Marcus debated whether to tell Bob about what he heard from Jay about Jake.

No. He wouldn't. It wasn't his secret to tell.

45

The next morning, Jason met Detective Ron Sanchez for breakfast. They had known each other for over ten years and agreed to an off-the-record meeting. They met in an obscure hash house in Oceanside, thirty miles from downtown San Diego, just to avoid the chance of anyone from the San Diego police force seeing them together.

"So," Jason said after they ordered. "Do you really think Isaacson is guilty? What about Maggie Garner?"

"Well, it would have been nice if we had had the dead guy's diaries sooner. But we didn't. And I'm assuming you turned them over in a timely manner."

"Scout's Honor."

"So . . ." Sanchez hesitated.

"So you're going to investigate Margaret Garner?" Jason asked.

"Yes. But I don't know. Her affair with Silver was a long time ago. You really think she could have sustained murderous rage for that long? Years? It's a stretch."

"Not when you add in the daughter."

Sanchez scowled. "Yeah. The daughter. I suppose we'll both be talking to her."

"I mean look," Jason went on, "the case against Isaacson is weak. You don't even have the murder weapon. Someone saw him go into the building? So what. He works there."

"I know. But this is a high profile case and . . ."

"And the boss wanted an arrest to kick the case off the front page."

"You said it, I didn't."

"I'm so glad I'm not a cop anymore." Jason drained his cup, though the coffee was miserable, and signaled to the waitress that they needed refills.

"What, you miss the long hours, the politics, and miserable pay?"

Jason laughed. "And eating in places like this. Oh, yeah. Big time."

"What about the wife?" Sanchez asked after taking a bite of his pancakes.

"Well, she's a cool customer, no question. Not exactly your typical wife. But the diaries paint a picture of a loving couple. This guy seems to have had it both ways, and she went along. Not so unusual. Just an extreme case, maybe."

"Yeah, but maybe she got fed up. First Garner, then the daughter. Might have made her snap."

"I don't get that vibe from her. At all. I assume you've looked into her?"

"Oh, yeah. Nothing."

"Well, there you go."

"Yet. Nothing yet."

46

Later that day, Jason and Marcus interviewed yet another of Chuck's casual affairs, and yet again, the woman in question, a La Jolla socialite with a breathtaking beachfront house, had an alibi for the time of Chuck's death.

"This is getting monotonous," Marcus said, driving Jason home on the way back to the city. "He was murdered Christmas week. Everyone was with people or out of town."

"I know. But that's how these cases go. You plug along and plug along and sooner or later, a pattern emerges, or something breaks."

"If you say so."

"I do. Trust me. So," Jason asked after a while. "How's it going at home?"

"Well, we're managing to keep things afloat. Bob's therapist wants me to come in for some joint sessions. We're going tomorrow."

"Maybe that's a good idea."

"Yeah, I guess. I just . . ."

"What?"

"I don't know. I wish . . ."

"You wish it hadn't happened."

"I wish it was eighteen years ago."

"When you first met."

"Yeah."

"And?"

"And I think we both just knew." Marcus felt an ache.

"Then it's not over. It's just different. Maybe just a little different."

"Thank you, Dr. Ruth."

They both laughed.

"Why don't you come for dinner," Marcus said. "I'm sure Bob is cooking. He's been cooking every night. I think he sees it as a kind of penance."

"Don't knock it. He's a great cook. But I have a date."

"Another marine? Or is it Navy this time?"

"Actually . . ."

"Yes?"

"It's with Joel Sanders."

"I beg your pardon? Run that by me again."

"I have a date with Joel Sanders."

Sanders, Marcus knew, was a rising star in the UCSD History department, and single. And handsome. Marcus couldn't have been more surprised if Jason had said he had a date with Tom Cruise.

"Where on earth did you two meet?"

"One night at Flicks," he smiled, mentioning the popular video bar in Hillcrest.

"You do know that he's not in the military? In fact, I'll bet he never has been. And he reads books. And writes them."

"Hey. I went to college, you know. I read. Some of the books don't even have pictures."

Marcus laughed.

"And besides," Jason added, "opposites attract."

"Okay, okay. Is this a first date?"

"Second, actually. First date was lunch. Last week."

"Lunch. The meal between breakfast and dinner? The one with little possibility of sex immediately following the meal?"

Jason laughed. "Yes. I've been known to eat lunch."

"And tonight is dinner? Where?"

"Oh, no. If I tell you, you and Bob will show up."

"Well, okay," Marcus said as he pulled off the freeway. "But I want a full report. Can I tell Bob?"

"Yes, you can tell Bob. Only Bob."

"Oh my God," was Bob's only reaction when Marcus told him as Bob was adding pepper to his fish stew on the stove.

47

The therapy appointment was at 8:00 the next morning, and they rushed to be on time after getting Lily off to school. She sensed something was different.

"What's happening?" she asked as they all wolfed down breakfast.

They looked at each other. "Nothing, sweetie, we're just both really busy at work today," Marcus said.

Lily didn't buy it, they could tell, but she let it go. So did they.

The therapist was David Drake, a gay man, who met clients at his home in Kensington, not far from their own house. He was a man of about forty with what Marcus thought of as typical California looks, tall, light brown hair, gym-toned body, dazzling smile. He had a diploma on the wall that showed a PhD in Psychology from UCLA. He had crafted a separate side entrance to his house for clients, with a small waiting room and an office with doors on both sides. It was simply but tastefully furnished.

He introduced himself, and Bob and Marcus arranged themselves on his couch. Marcus was tense; he didn't know what was coming. As he had contemplated this session in the last few days, he imagined everything from Bob's tearful apology to a break-up.

"Marcus," Drake began, "Bob knows, and I know, how difficult these last weeks have been for you."

Marcus gave a slight nod.

"He has some things he wants to say to you."

"First," Bob began, "I am grateful that you didn't leave, or kick me out, or make a scene that would have been so hard for Lily."

Marcus had been been facing straight forward, and now turned more toward Bob.

"Do you remember when I said this happened because I was lonely?"

"Yes." For a moment Marcus looked down at the blue-gray carpet. Low pile, very sensible, wouldn't show dirt, he thought out of nowhere.

"David helped me understand something. I wasn't feeling lonely with you. Or at home. I was feeling lonely because dad died so suddenly."

"Well, I can understand that. It was a shock."

They both looked at Drake.

"According to Freud," Drake said, "the death of a man's father is the most poignant moment in his life. Everyone reacts differently. In this case, there was no warning, no chance to say good-bye. And Bob and Jake were close. Unusually so, especially for a gay man and his father. That doesn't happen all that often."

"Yes, I know," Marcus said, thinking about his own father. "I was close to Jake as well. And I miss him, too."

Bob started to tear up. "I relied on him for so much. And it happened just as I was turning forty."

Marcus wanted to reach for Bob's hand, but he stopped himself. He didn't know if that would be considered inappropriate.

"And after he died, my drinking picked up. And I wanted more sex."

"Yes," Marcus said with a slight laugh, "I noticed."

"Both of those things are common reactions to a death such as this," Drake said.

"And then," Bob said, "I started to feel guilty for making so many demands on you."

That surprised Marcus. "You mean sexual demands?"

"Yes."

"Why would you feel guilty?" Marcus asked. He was truly surprised. "I mean, we've always had a healthy sex life. I've never turned you down, have I?"

"I know. You haven't. I can't really explain it. Maybe it wasn't rational. Or maybe I should have said something. But I felt guilty."

Both Drake and Marcus waited.

"And there was something else," Bob said. "Something I haven't told you. Just before Dad died, the day before, in fact, Anna told me she was thinking about leaving the firm. She had gotten an offer from a bigger firm in LA."

"What?" Marcus said. He was genuinely shocked.

"Yes. It felt like everyone was leaving me, I just couldn't cope.

And then I met Derrick at that New Year's Eve party, and he invited me to have a drink." He paused.

"Go on," Drake urged.

"And I drank too much. And he was so damn good-looking, it just happened. I didn't plan it or go looking for it. And I thought, stupidly, maybe it would be better to work out this crazy sex thing with a stranger rather than pestering you so much. I know that sounds like an excuse. But I just wasn't thinking. I was just . . . crazed. Not myself."

Marcus let that sink in for a long moment.

"Marcus," Drake asked, "do you have anything you want to ask, or say?"

"That day I saw you in the restaurant, it looked like the two of you were . . ."

"Were what?" Drake asked. "You can be honest here. That's the point."

"You looked happy."

"I wasn't happy at all. I was miserable. I was putting on a show. You know, like I do in court. It was an act."

"It didn't look like an act," Marcus said, as gently as he could.

"That's why I'm a good lawyer. Dad taught me that. In fact, when I was just starting out, I used to have practice sessions with Dad in front of a mirror. He taught me to hide my feelings in court. Sometimes you have to. Judges, juries, they notice everything. Every tiny movement. You have to be an actor."

"I can believe that."

"You remember when I worked for the DA? That mess?"

"Yes, of course."

"I would never have gotten through that without Dad. And he always gave me advice on cases when I needed it. So it wasn't just a personal loss. I felt so . . . alone. I don't mean with you. I mean out there, in the world. I wasn't sure I could be a good lawyer without him, and without Anna."

Marcus nodded.

"I didn't care about Derrick at all. I didn't even like him, to tell the truth. And the sex felt . . . empty. It only happened twice. I was already planning to end it."

There was a long pause.

"And," Bob added, "I don't want to lose you."

Now it was Marcus's turn to tear up. "I don't want to lose you either."

Drake had them talk about some of their best times together. They both agreed that their very best day was the day they brought Lily home. And they talked about the early days, in Cambridge, when Bob was a law student and would stay up half the night studying and then crawl into bed with Marcus.

And then the hour was up. They agreed to have at least one more session, and that night, they fell asleep facing each other.

"Would Anna really leave?" Marcus asked, as he drifted off. "That would be awful."

"No. She's staying. Thank God."

48

Two days later, Jason and Marcus had lunch. "So, how was the date?" Marcus asked.

"Most satisfactory."

"And?"

"And I learned that professors have penises. But you already knew that."

Marcus laughed.

"We're interviewing Danielle Garner in Los Angeles on Saturday."

"We? Can't you do this one alone? She's not an academic. You don't need me."

"It's something I learned when I was a cop. Witnesses, suspects, always feel better when talking to two people instead of one. I need you there. You know, we play good cop, bad cop, if we need to. Cagney and Lacey did it all the time." That had been a very popular TV series in the 1980s about two female police detectives.

"Ok, but I get to be Cagney." Lacey was a Queens housewife. That wasn't me, Marcus thought.

"Why do you get to be Cagney?"

"If I don't get to be Cagney, I'm not coming."

"Okay, Okay."

That evening he told Bob about going to LA, who suggested they go together and spend the night with Alex and Carol. "Maybe mom can come up too. Lily can play with Ruthie," Bob said hopefully.

Marcus agreed. Things were feeling back to normal.

They drove up on Saturday morning. Traffic was heavy when they got to the outskirts of Los Angeles, as it always was, but they finally arrived around noon. Ruth was already there from Laguna Beach, and everyone seemed to be in a good mood. To their surprise, Jay was home for the weekend.

After a quick lunch Marcus left to meet Jason. As he left the house, he heard Lily say, "So who wants to play cards?" Jay groaned.

Danielle Garner lived in a small but upscale studio apartment in Westwood, near the UCLA campus. She looked very much like a younger version of her mother, only she had lightened her hair. She opened the door barefoot, wearing shorts and a blouse with several buttons provocatively undone. She offered them coffee which they both declined. They sat on the small, garishly pink loveseat. She perched on the edge of the double bed.

Jason began. "We've been asked by Emma Baker to look into the death of her husband."

Danielle nodded.

"We understand you had a relationship with him."

"Yes, we were fucking."

She watched to see if they would flinch at the word. They didn't.

"Where would you meet?"

"At his place near the beach. Or here."

"And how often did you get together?"

"About once a month."

"Mr. Silver kept a journal. Some of the entries suggest he wanted to break off the relationship but that you did not want to end it."

She got up and poured herself a cup of coffee from the small galley kitchen.

"You could say that. It was good sex. I didn't want it to end." She was clearly enjoying what she assumed would shock them.

"Had you been aware that Mr. Silver had had a previous relationship with your mother?"

"He told me as much. I wasn't surprised."

"Why is that?"

"My mother had told me . . . no, hinted, really, that she and my dear old dad no longer had a physical relationship."

"I see."

"Where did you meet Mr. Silver?"

"At an art exhibition in Laguna. We started talking and realized we had a La Jolla connection."

"Were you angry that Mr. Silver wanted things to cool down?"

"Not angry, no. I mean, this is Los Angeles. I'm at UCLA. It's always possible to get laid." She smiled. "But I wanted it to go on."

"For the record, where were you on Friday, December 27th?"

"I knew you'd ask me that." She handed them a piece of paper with a name, address, and phone number. "I was in San Francisco with a friend from school."

"Thank you for that. Did Mr. Silver ever say anything that might be a clue to who killed him? Did he ever mention an enemy, anything like that? Any trouble he was having?"

"Well, I knew Mom was furious with him. And she's a bitch. Nothing would surprise me about her."

Jason and Marcus both did their best not to look surprised.

"And do you think your mother is capable of murder?"

"I'll leave that to you boys to figure out." Marcus suddenly realized that Danielle was staring at Jason's crotch.

"One more question. Have the San Diego police interviewed you? Did you tell them all this?"

"Yep."

"Well, thank you for your time."

"Any time, boys." She held the door open for them.

"Now that," Jason said out on the street, "is quite a family."

"Yeah," Marcus said. "Like the Addams family. Without the humor."

49

Ruth and Bob prepared an elaborate dinner of grilled tuna steak, roasted vegetables, and couscous. Carol had baked a cherry pie. Everyone seemed to be in a good mood. After dinner, Ruth suggested Lily and Ruthie watch television in the den. She closed the door after they settled there and gathered everyone else in the living room.

"I want to talk," she said.

"Mom, are you okay?" Alex asked, anxious.

"Yes, I'm fine. Of course I miss your father. But I'm coping. I'm going to a bereavement group. It helps."

That was news to everyone.

"I want to talk about something else. What happened at Bob's birthday party, and the aftermath."

"Maybe we should let it go," Bob said.

"No, I don't think so. Jay overheard something. He was upset. That's understandable. We need to talk about it."

Everyone looked at Jay. He looked down.

"So he and I talked," Ruth added.

That was news to Carol and Alex, who looked again at Jay. Ruth went on.

"I wanted him to understand that most marriages hit bumps. Sometimes that bump is an affair."

Both Bob and Alex looked away.

Ruth went on. "I know this will be hard to hear, boys. But it happened to us. To your father and me."

"What??" Alex said, turning back to look at his mother. Bob was too shocked to say anything. He looked down at the floor.

"You boys were quite young. I was so busy with you, with the new house, with everything. I was exhausted all the time. Your father had that big case in federal court, and he thought he was going to lose, even though he won in the end. He was sure that his law practice depended on the outcome of that case. He was hardly ever home. Sometimes he stayed overnight in Hartford when things got really complex. You remember that, don't you?"

Alex did and said so. Bob was too young.

"Look. All I'm saying is, it happens. Even when people love each other and are happy together."

"And you forgave him?" Alex asked.

"Yes."

Alex got up and fetched glasses and a bottle of brandy. He offered it around, and only Carol took some.

"This isn't the kind of family conference they had on *Ozzie and Harriet*," he said.

"Well, maybe they should have," Bob said. "Little Ricky was pretty screwed up. In real life." Everyone smiled.

"Look," Ruth went on. "Here's the point. I know a good marriage when I see one. Your father and I had one. You know that. And so do all of you. Not you, Jay, not yet. But if you're as lucky as your father and uncle, and as smart, you'll find one."

Everyone smiled. Carol put her hand on top of her son's.

"And, by the way, I want great-grandchildren before I go," Ruth added.

"Um," Jay said, turning pale, "May I have some of that brandy?"

50

On Monday, Jay popped into Marcus's office on campus at noon. He asked if he was free for lunch, and once again they went to the faculty club.

"So, are you forgiving Bob?" Jay asked after they fetched their plates. He had clearly picked up the family trait of speaking frankly.

"Yes. Working my way there."

"Good. I'm glad. I don't want to lose you."

"I'm glad too," Marcus said, and smiled. "And you've forgiven your father?"

"Yeah, mostly. I figure if mom can, I can. And there's Ruthie to think about."

"Yes. Good."

"Grandma Ruth is quite a lady," Jay said, tearing a piece of bread.

"Yes, she is. A rock. Like your mother."

"You're right. I never really thought of it that way, but they're a lot alike." He still looked a little troubled.

"But?"

"The great-grandchildren thing. That freaked me out. I mean, medical school, it's a long haul. Really long."

"Of course. But she'll probably live to be ninety-five. You have time."

Jay laughed. "And the thing is . . ."

"Hmm?"

"Um, my sexuality is a little fluid right now."

Marcus was surprised, but not shocked. "Well," he said, "that's only natural. You're figuring yourself out. That's part of college. A big part of it."

"Yeah. And the thing is, when you and Uncle Bob adopted Lily, that really meant a lot to me. Showed me what can happen."

Marcus felt really touched. He waited to see if Jay would add any more details about himself, but he didn't, and Marcus didn't want to press him.

They turned to small talk. As they left the club, Rudd Martin waved to Marcus.

"Who is that guy? With the scarf?" Jay asked.

"Oh, Professor Martin. In the French department."

"Figures," Jay said.

"He's not gay, if that's what you're thinking. At least, I don't think so."

"Hmm" was Jay's only reply.

51

That afternoon, word reached Marcus via Jason that the murder charge against Fred Isaacson had been dropped, without prejudice, meaning the charges could conceivably be refiled later. But, in the meantime, the police still had found no trace of the murder weapon. The eyewitness who supposedly saw Fred go into the building that day admitted in her deposition, under hard questioning from Fred's attorney, that she couldn't be sure it was Fred. And Chuck's diaries made clear that, while he and Chuck were intellectual foes and rivals, they were also on friendly terms. Emma gave a deposition saying the same thing.

"Isaacson's attorney did his job," Jason said.

"So where does that leave the investigation?"

"I spoke to Emma. She's more determined than ever to find the perp. We need to press on. She wants us to talk to as many of Silver's women as possible. I think in some way she thinks if we talk to them, they don't count anymore. That's not rational, I know. But I've seen this kind of thing before."

Marcus sighed. "And the police?"

"They're turning their attention to Maggie Garner. And her daughter."

Sure enough, a few days later, the police exercised a search warrant of Maggie Garner's home and office. The search of the office on campus produced a buzz in record time; within 24 hours, everyone knew about the search and that Maggie Garner was a murder suspect.

She went into seclusion for a day. Then, the following morning, she put out a statement, saying she was stepping down temporarily as Senior Vice Chancellor, "for personal reasons." The chair of the Chemistry department, who had been serving as her assistant, was appointed Acting SVC in her place. The statement was terse and said nothing about the murder investigation. Reporters camped out on campus and in front of her home, and she started wearing dark glasses. Rumor was that her husband left town, but that turned out not to be true.

"We need to go to Ann Arbor and New York," Jason said in their next phone call.

"Can we do it during Spring break? It's a few weeks away."

"Yeah, I suppose. In the meantime, we'll see if the police turn up anything."

They did. Maggie and George Garner kept a gun in their home, registered to George. It was found in a safe at their home, and it was the same caliber as the gun that killed Charles Silver.

52

George Garner, like Maggie, had been out of town on the day Chuck Silver died, so the police were digging into their phone and financial records, and questioning them repeatedly, to see if one or both of them might have hired a hit man. Photographers were still stationed in front of their home. Maggie hardly ever left the house.

Meanwhile the case was back in the news, and reporters uncovered the affair between Maggie and Chuck Silver, which was splashed across the front page and led the local TV news for a few nights. Marcus suspected Emma had leaked the story and suggested to Jason that they ask her if she did, but Jason talked him out of it.

The University administration was apoplectic about the publicity and worried it would impact fundraising and the campus's long-term reputation. It was whispered that the Chancellor wanted to fire Maggie from her administrative post, but was talked out of it by the campus counsel; it could have led to a lawsuit and more bad publicity if charges were never filed, the campus lawyer said. The Chancellor, who was rumored to be in line for the UC presidency, complied, reluctantly. He also, apparently, had political ambitions, and the UC presidency would be a huge stepping stone. He didn't want to risk anything.

Maggie and George each had their own attorney. Marcus thought that was strange, but Bob explained that that was a smart strategy in cases like this, where both spouses were suspects in a murder, or any serious crime.

"Like in the Jon-Benet Ramsey case," Bob said. Ramsey, a young girl, had been found dead in her home in Boulder, and both parents were suspects.

Time passed, but no charges were filed against either Garner. Jason speculated that the ballistics or fingerprint report on the gun might have been inconclusive.

Soon it was almost Spring break.

"Do we really need this trip?" Marcus asked Jason. He really was sick of being mixed up in the investigation, especially since it didn't seem to be going anywhere, and he just wanted to relax over break—and perhaps spend some quality time with Bob.

"I don't think either Garner did this," Jason said. "As you said, she had a lot to lose. Her affair with Silver was in the past. And apparently the marriage was over in all but name, so why would George do it? It doesn't make a lot of sense. At least not yet."

"So, back to the snowbelt?" Marcus asked.

"Well, it's March, won't the snow be gone?" Jason said, hopefully.

"In New York, probably. Ann Arbor, no."

Jason's secretary made the travel arrangements, and that night Marcus told Bob about the trip. He also realized he had never told him about his lunch with Jay, what with all the excitement about Maggie Garner and the usual crush of mid-semester work. He debated whether he should say anything, and finally decided he would.

"Wow," Bob said. "I mean, I never really thought about it, but . . . wow."

"Yeah."

"In high school, Jay didn't have a girlfriend exactly," Bob said, "more like five or six close friends, male and female. They were sort of like a pack."

"Do you think they were . . ."

"I don't know what they were. They might not have known either."

"True."

"Do you think he's talked to Alex and Carol about it?" Bob asked.

"I don't think so, since he's not sure what's what. At least, that's my guess. When Ruth talked about great-grandchildren . . ."

"Yeah. I could see that freaked him out. So he's thinking about all of it. I'll find out what he's doing over Spring break. Maybe see him if I can."

"He said something about surfing lessons over break," Marcus said.

"Oh, God. I hope he doesn't break his neck."

On Sunday morning, Bob dropped Marcus and Jason off at the airport for their flight to Detroit.

53

Their flight landed at 6:00 p.m. local time. It was 35 degrees and there was indeed dirty snow on the ground.

"Well," Jason said, "at least it's not as bad as Chicago."

They took the shuttle to Ann Arbor, which took about forty-five minutes, and checked into the nondescript, tall, concrete Campus Inn. Jet-lagged, they weren't ready for dinner until around 9:30.

Marcus had been an undergraduate at the University and took Jason to one of his favorite restaurants, a diner where, much to his surprise, he ran into one of his college classmates, who had gone on to get a PhD in political science and was now on the faculty. They recognized each other immediately, even though they hadn't seen each other for almost thirty years.

"Marcus George, look at you!"

"Jim Pierce. Good God."

They hugged and chatted for a bit and then Pierce had to be on his way, and Marcus turned back to Jason and the menu.

"Were you two . . . you know . . ." Jason asked, suggestively.

"Jim? Oh God no. He's straight as they come."

"He seemed awfully happy to see you. You never . . ."

"I was always in the library. And you are turning into a dirty old man."

Jason laughed.

Their appointment with Eve Jacobs wasn't until 1:00 the next afternoon, so they slept late the next morning, had a leisurely breakfast, and then Marcus took a walk around the town and campus alone.

He stopped at the undergraduate library, universally called the UGLI, which had been expanded and upgraded since his days there and now even had a snack bar. In Marcus's time, there was only a machine in the basement dispensing bad coffee; Marcus had been there almost every night. He lingered, watching the studying undergrads, most with their laptops in front of them, a far cry from the pencils and pens and notebooks of his undergraduate years.

Then he strolled over to the huge graduate library, where he had been given a coveted study carrel when he was writing his honors thesis as a senior. He peered into the fourth-floor carrel, which was empty, and remembered the view out the window over the town.

"Was I ever that young?" he murmured to himself as he left.

He wandered through some of the classroom buildings, feeling both happy and sad, remembering friends, good friends back then, now mostly lost. He had done his best to stay in touch with some of them, and that worked for a few years.

And then everyone's life took over.

He walked all the way to the dorm he had lived in for two years, Mosher-Jordan. A fierce wind was blowing. It was a long walk that he used to do two, sometimes three times a day without giving it a thought; now, at fifty, it tired him out. He stepped into one of the front lounges where he used to sit with a book, sometimes late into the night. A fire had been lit in the old stone fireplace, and a few students were reading, talking. Some looked up, then ignored him.

Then he walked over to the house he shared with some friends for his last two years, which was near the Inn. It too had been expanded, and, as he stood in front of it, he almost started to cry. It had been home, more home than his home in Chicago at the time.

A student came out the front door, the one that led to the second and third floor, where their apartment had been.

"Can I help you?" he asked.

"No, I'm just in town for a day, and I used to live here."

"Wow, really? When?"

"In the mid-seventies."

"Would you like to come in, look around?"

Marcus was tempted, but said no. "Thanks, though, that's kind of you."

They walked together down State Street.

"Where do you live now?"

"San Diego."

"Nice. Must be warm."

Marcus smiled. "Yes. Palm trees and sunshine."

It was a short walk to the hotel and Marcus turned, but he stopped to watch the student continue down State Street, on a path he had walked countless times. From the back, Marcus thought, that could have been me. It seemed . . . like yesterday. Such a cliché, he knew. But that was the thing about a cliché. It was a cliché because it was often true.

He picked up Jason and they had a quick lunch at another restaurant Marcus used to go to when he could afford it; it was bustling with students chattering away. Most of them looked like they didn't have a care in the world. Then it was time for their appointment.

54

They had arranged to meet Eve Jacobs in her office in the central administration building; she had recently been appointed a special assistant to the university president. The building was an ugly, brown brick square with small windows. It had been built in the late 1960s, at a time of student demonstrations, and was clearly built to prevent student takeovers or window-smashing. From the outside, it could have passed for a municipal jail.

They found Jacobs in her office on the second floor. They both immediately saw that she closely resembled Emma, though somewhat younger; they guessed around thirty-five. She was wearing a tailored apricot-colored suit and high heels.

She shook their hands and offered coffee or tea. Jason

accepted a cup of tea.

"So, gentlemen, I understand you are here to talk about Chuck Silver. What can I tell you?" She sounded businesslike and emotion-free.

"Yes, thank you for seeing us," Jason said. "How would you characterize your relationship with Mr. Silver?"

"We had known each other casually through conferences, that sort of thing. Then we tried to recruit him to our English department. I was Associate Chair of that department at the time, so I was point-person of the recruitment effort, more or less."

That was startling to Marcus, although, as he thought about it for a moment, he realized it wasn't surprising at all; Chuck was an academic star.

"Was he receptive to the offer?" Marcus asked. He surprised himself by jumping into the questioning so quickly.

"Well, he didn't say no right away, which we found encouraging."

"And what about his spouse?" Marcus asked.

"That was one of the negotiating points. Chuck made it clear from the beginning he would not leave UCSD without a tenured position for Emma. It took some time, and a lot of persuasion, but the French department here finally agreed."

"How long did the negotiations last?" Jason asked.

"A full academic year, four years ago."

"And was that the extent of your relationship during that time?"

Eve Jacobs got up, went to a side table, and poured herself a cup of water.

"Chuck visited the campus several times over the course of that year. We became close."

"Intimate?" Jason asked.

"Yes. You see, I was going through a divorce at the time. And

Chuck said he and Emma had an understanding."

"And then?"

"And then he turned down the job offer, even though we kept sweetening the deal, and the relationship ended."

"I see," Jason said. "Mr. Silver, it turns out, kept a journal. A diary. In it, there are various suggestions that you did not want the relationship to end."

"Well," Jacobs said, staring out her narrow window, "there's some truth in that. Chuck was a very engaging man, for all sorts of reasons. But eventually I came to my senses." She smiled.

"I see. For the record, where were you on Friday, December 27th? That's the day Mr. Silver was murdered. Were you at the San Diego convention?"

"I was there briefly on Thursday morning for the meeting of a journal editorial board, then Thursday evening I flew to Atlanta to spend New Year's with some friends. I can get you the travel receipt."

"Just to be thorough, that would be helpful," Jason said.

"Of course." She buzzed her secretary, who, after a moment, brought in a folder that contained an airline ticket receipt and a hotel bill.

"Is there anything else?"

"Did you have the sense that Emma was receptive to moving?" Marcus asked. He wasn't sure why, but he wanted to know.

"Emma visited only once. I didn't get much sense of her, either way. She gave the impression . . ."

"Yes?"

"I got the sense she thought we were beneath her. Not the university, but the location. The Midwest."

Marcus understood what Jacobs was saying. To coastal elites, the Midwest was flat, boring, uncultured. A backwater. He had heard the refrain, real or implied, many times, having been born in Chicago and not having attended a coastal undergraduate college or university.

"Well," Jason said, "thank you for your time."

"Not at all. I hope this murder gets solved."

55

"Well," Jason said as they walked in a fierce wind back to their hotel, "another dead end."

"Yeah."

"Tell me," Jason said. "Why are there so many academic types who are so casual about affairs? I thought you guys were a pretty straight-laced bunch."

"Well," Marcus said, "we're hardly seeing a representative sample."

"I guess that's right," Jason said.

"But for what it's worth," Marcus went on, "I've been wondering if there isn't some kind of connection. And all I can think of is that great literature is full of depictions of all sorts of relationships, all sorts of attraction. I mean, dozens of great novels deal with adultery. Others deal with sexual obsession. It's always been one of the great literary themes."

"Huh. And?"

"And maybe that makes some folks aware of the possibilities. So to speak. It makes some more cautious. Like me."

Jason smiled.

"And it makes others . . ."

"It turns others into Chuck Silver," Jason offered. "I mean, I don't know if that explains him. Maybe he was amoral. Maybe he was a sex addict. It sounds to me like maybe he was. Or maybe the explanation for his behavior was his own psychology, some sense of inadequacy he was trying to overcome, and had nothing to do with his academic subject. Who knows."

Jason did not reply, but Marcus could see that he was thinking.

They checked out of the Campus Inn and caught the shuttle to the Detroit airport for their flight to New York. As the van pulled out of town, Marcus wondered if he would ever see it again, and closed his eyes.

56

Their flight was delayed, so they sat in the airport coffee shop. Jason looked through the local newspaper while Marcus read an impenetrable analysis of modern rhetoric, written by a professor at Duke, where, Marcus was sure, it was an institutional requirement to write in obscure language that only ten initiated individuals on the planet would understand.

Finally their flight was announced. There was freezing rain, and, as they boarded, the outside of the plane was being de-iced, which made Jason wince. After the short flight it was warmer in New York and raining when they landed, around 50 degrees, but a wet wind was blowing in off New York harbor. Jason shivered.

They found a cab and got to their midtown Manhattan hotel around 6:30 and checked in. Marcus called home and spoke first to Bob and then to Lily, who told him all about her boring day at school.

"Dad, maybe I should just go straight to high school," she said.

"Um, sweet pea, we'll talk about that when I get home. Put Pop back on, okay?"

"Did you hear that?" Marcus asked.

"Yeah," Bob whispered. "We have got to get her into the

Academy. I'll call, find out what the process involves."

Marcus and Jason then took the subway to Chelsea, which had rapidly replaced the West Village as the neighborhood of choice for gay men, who were everywhere on the street.

"Now this," Jason said as they emerged from the subway and looked around, "is what I call a target-rich environment."

Marcus laughed. "What about your historian?"

"Early days. But promising."

They stopped for a drink at one gay bar, where the crowd immediately sized up Jason. A young hunk came over and started chatting him up, so Marcus made himself scarce; he walked over to a corner and nursed his bottle of mineral water. He watched Jason and admired his nonchalance, his smile, his everything. He was relaxed in a way Marcus had never been in a gay bar, even when he was young and single.

After a while Jason rejoined Marcus.

"I can go have dinner alone if you want to . . . you know . . . explore options," Marcus suggested with a smile.

"No, he was way too young."

"That's never stopped you with the Marine Corps," Marcus teased.

"I know. But I'm not as young as I used to be, you know. And he was an airhead. All he wanted to talk about was video games."

"Ah, well, you can't have everything."

They walked out and wandered around a bit, finally stopping at a chic-looking bistro for dinner. There were lots of glances in their direction.

"I guess we're fresh meat," Jason said.

"You, maybe. I'm leftovers."

The meal was mediocre and overpriced. After dinner, Jason wanted to hit another bar.

"Okay, but I'm going back to the hotel soon. I'm way too old for all this."

They walked into another place, packed and overheated. Jason went to the crowded bar to get their drinks, and, while Jason waited for the bartender to notice him, Marcus heard a voice to his side.

"Professor George, what are you doing here?!"

The smooth voice belonged to a rather corporate type, and Marcus realized he had been one of his students years ago at Harvard, when he had just started teaching.

"Steven?" He paused, grasping for the name. "Steven . . . Blake! Good grief, how are you?"

"I'm fine. What are you doing in New York? I heard you moved to California."

"I did. San Diego. I'm just here for a day or two."

Blake was wearing an expensive looking suit and had loosened his silk tie. He had an executive-style haircut and looked well manicured from head to toe, the picture of a sophisticated New York gay man.

"And I heard you hooked up with a law student at Harvard. Are you still together?"

"Yes, we are. Eighteen years now. And we have a daughter."

"Wow. That's great."

"So what are you doing these days, Steven?"

"I'm in investment banking. After Harvard I went to business school. Columbia."

"How is it?"

"Well, the money's good." He let out a little laugh. "And New York is really expensive. It's kinda insane."

"Yes, I've noticed."

For a moment they both listened to the thumping music. Jason had gotten their drinks but was standing off to the side, watching, with an amused look on his face. After a while, Steven spoke.

"You know, Professor George, I always had a little crush on you at Harvard."

Marcus turned red. "Really?" He was flabbergasted.

"Yeah. In fact a bunch of us did. We used to talk about it sometimes. I mean, for one thing, you were one of the few who didn't try to hide being gay back then."

Steven took a big gulp of his drink. Marcus didn't know what to say. It was true; most of the other gay faculty at the time, the early 1980s, were closeted, or very, very circumspect at places like Harvard.

"Yeah. And I kinda always dug older guys. Still do." Steve was staring hard at Marcus, who was beginning to feel uncomfortable, and, at the same time, to his great surprise, aroused.

"Would you like to make my fantasy real tonight," Steven said, seductively, smiling.

For a brief moment, Marcus's body was saying yes.

"Um, I appreciate the offer, but the thing is, my partner and I, we don't fool around on each other."

"After eighteen years?" Steven was incredulous.

"I know, it sounds like we're from the nineteenth century."

"No, no. I get it. Really. But you can't blame a guy for trying."

"No. Of course not."

"Take care, Professor George. It was good seeing you."

"You too, Steven. Be well."

Steven walked off and disappeared into the crowd. Jason joined Marcus.

"Now don't tell me," Jason said, "you weren't tempted."

"I was. For a split second."

"But."

"Yes, but. I'm going to go back to the hotel. You can stay if you want."

"I think I will. Who knows when I'll ever be in New York

again," he said, scanning the crowd.

Marcus smiled on his way back to the hotel. He took a shower and crawled into bed.

57

They were awakened the next morning by bright sun streaming through the hotel window and the sound of garbage trucks.

Marcus yawned and looked over at Jason.

"So," he asked, "did you get lucky last night?"

"Nah. I got back soon after you. You were sound asleep."

"I don't know if I believe that."

Jason laughed. They took turns taking showers and ordered continental breakfast, which came with *The New York Times*. There was a front-page story about how John Kerry now had the Democratic presidential nomination wrapped up.

"Can he win?" Jason asked.

"God, I hope so. My brother seems to think he can."

Their appointment with Jennifer Lindsey at Columbia was at 11:00. They took the subway to Morningside Heights and met her in her office in a modern, nondescript building.

Lindsey was a beautiful blonde of about forty, immaculately dressed in a khaki-colored pant suit with a dark blue scarf. Clearly, professional women these days were all wearing pant suits. Marcus wondered if they had Hillary Clinton to thank for that.

They took chairs around a small conference table in front of her office window. The table held the page proofs of a manuscript Marcus assumed was a new piece of Lindsey's scholarship. Marcus noticed the title, "The Hermeneutics of Colonial Identity."

"So, gentlemen, I assume you're here about Chuck Silver?"

"Yes. We've been asked to look into his murder by his widow,"

Jason said.

"I assumed as much."

"Mr. Silver kept a journal, and it appears from some of the entries that you and he were involved."

"Yes, we were." She looked down.

"How did you meet?"

"At a conference, about six years ago."

"And how often did you meet?"

"Not often. It probably amounted to something like twice a year."

"And how long did it go on?"

"On and off for about three years or so. It was very casual."

"And how did it end?"

"Well . . . at one point we were about to get together, but Chuck wasn't feeling well. And then after that, I'd say Emma put her foot down."

"Oh?" Jason said.

"Yes. I'm guessing, but that was my impression."

"Can you elaborate?"

She got up to pour herself a glass of water from a pitcher on her desk. Marcus noticed it was crystal.

"When it started, Chuck told me that he and Emma had an understanding, which I took to me they had an open marriage. Lots of couples do these days."

"So what changed?"

"I'm really not sure. You'd have to ask Emma."

"Forgive me for asking this, but did you try to prolong the affair?"

"No, not really. I did confront Chuck and ask him what had changed, and he was rather tongue-tied, which was unusual for him. Very unusual."

"I see. And did he say anything specific about Emma when

you confronted him?"

"No, not really. To tell the truth it was a rather disjointed conversation on both sides. We were in a bar in Chicago, after a conference. I think we both had had too much to drink."

"I see. For the record, were you at the MLA in December?"

"No, I didn't go this year."

"So you were here in New York?"

"Yes."

"Can anyone corroborate that?"

"Am I a murder suspect?" she said with a little laugh.

"We're just trying to be thorough."

"All right." She got up, went to her desk, and looked at a large calendar.

"What day did Chuck die?"

"Friday the twenty-seventh."

"On Wednesday of that week, Christmas Day, I had dinner with my mother and father. On Thursday I had lunch with a colleague and dinner with some friends, a married couple. On Friday I had lunch with another colleague. Would you like those names?"

"Please."

She wrote down names and addresses and phone numbers on notebook paper and handed it to Jason, who noticed she had very precise handwriting.

"Is there anything else? Would you like a DNA sample, or blood, perhaps?"

Marcus turned red and Jason smiled. "No, that won't be necessary. Thank you for seeing us."

"Not at all." She closed her office door after them.

"Interesting that she thinks Emma put her foot down," Jason said as they walked to the subway.

"Yes. Very. But I wonder if it's true," Marcus said.

"You think it isn't?"

"I don't know. But I can imagine it's what she told herself, instead of believing Chuck lost interest."

"Yeah, that's possible. But this one seems to have lasted longer than most. That could have gotten to Emma."

"True."

"We'll need to ask her about it."

They got back to their hotel, checked out, and took a cab to the airport.

58

O n the long flight home, Jason dozed and Marcus finished reading his book, understanding very little of it. He kept looking out the window. Marcus always enjoyed flying west at this time of day, prolonging the light. It felt like cheating nature.

It was 7:00 when they landed. They shared a cab and dropped Marcus off at home.

"I'll set something up with Emma," Jason said. Marcus frowned, and then smiled when he heard Jason give the driver his own home address.

Lily ran to the door and threw her arms around her father.

"Daddy!"

"Hey, sweet pea." He brushed the back of her head and then leaned down to cuddle an excited Zelda. Bob came in from the kitchen and they kissed.

"There's leftover quiche if you're hungry."

"Actually I am. The airplane food was the usual muck."

In the kitchen Bob put the quiche in the microwave and Marcus poured himself a tall glass of iced tea. Long flights always left him parched.

"So how's school?"

"It's so boring," Lily said.

"It can't all be boring," Marcus said.

"Well, music and art are fun. But everything else, yuck. It's too easy."

Marcus glanced at Bob.

"Well, sweet pea," Bob said, "we may be able to get you into a school that won't be so boring."

"Really?" She was excited.

"Yes. We have to go talk to them together, and they'll want you to take a few tests."

"That's okay, I'm really good at tests."

Bob laughed. "Yes, we know."

Marcus dug into the quiche, which was delicious.

"There's salad too, although it's probably soggy."

"No, this is fine."

Marcus got up and put the kettle on for more tea. They all sat in the living room for a while. Bob was working on a case, papers strewn around him, and Marcus read the local news until it was time to tuck Lily in bed. He was jet-lagged and collapsed in the master bedroom.

"So tell me about the school," he said to Bob when he walked in.

"It's impressive. Everything. The building, the teachers. And they have space for Lily. Good timing. Expensive."

"Yeah, I figured it would be. But we have her trust fund. It should be enough to cover it, and college, and grad school, if it comes to that."

When they had adopted Lily, Ruth and Jake had set up a trust fund for her, as they had for Jay and for Ruthie. Bob and Marcus had added to it, and they got good financial advice about where to invest it.

"You look beat," Bob said.

"I am. All the running around. And jet lag."

"Are you getting anywhere on the case?"

"No. Not at all."

Bob sat at the edge of the bed and started massaging Marcus's stockinged feet.

"Oh God, that feels amazing."

"By the way, Jay wants to stay over for a few nights before the end of break."

"Sure. Where is he now?"

"He went home for a few days and is coming back, tomorrow I think. He says a friend is teaching him to surf."

"Oy."

"The thing is . . ."

"What?"

"I think this may be a special friend."

"Ah."

"Does the friend want to stay over too?"

"No, his parents live here."

"Does this entity have a name?"

"Rick."

Marcus smiled. "All gay men . . ."

Bob finished the sentence. "Are named Mark or Rick or Steve."

They laughed. It felt good to laugh together.

"Why don't you take a hot shower and turn in. Anna's coming over."

"Now??"

"Yeah, we have to finish a brief. It needed some research, so she's been at the law library. We lost our clerk, he had to go home, some family emergency in Nebraska. She said she'd stop over on her way home. It shouldn't take long."

"Okay." Marcus hauled himself up. "Thanks for the foot job."

"Anytime. My rates are quite reasonable."

59

The next morning, Jason called at 10:00. He had heard from Detective Sanchez, off the record, that the police were about to make an arrest for Chuck's murder.

"Did he say who?"

"No."

"Did you alert Emma?"

"Yes."

"Any idea who?"

"Well, I'd guess one of the Garners, or both."

Bob had left for his office, Lily was at school, and, for once, Zelda was not demanding a morning walk, so Marcus sat down at the desk in his study and tried to concentrate on the article he was writing. It was little use; he couldn't stop wondering what the news would be. And he couldn't get the convoluted Duke book out of his head.

Just before noon, the phone rang again. Jason.

"They've arrested Maggie Garner for first-degree murder."

"Oh, God. Apart from having a gun in the house, do you think they have any evidence?"

"Well they must have found something."

"I wonder," Marcus said.

"I spoke to Emma. She's skeptical. Like you, she thinks Maggie had too much to lose."

"That's interesting."

"Yes."

"Did you ask her about Lindsey?"

"Yes. She claims Chuck got tired of her, like all the rest. She claims she had nothing to do with the end of the affair."

"Huh. There's no way to really know, is there? I mean, Emma could be trying to avoid embarrassment."

"That's possible."

By 1:00, the phone was ringing off the hook, colleagues from campus, and some from around the country, wanting to know what Marcus knew about Maggie's arrest. Over and over, he told them. "Nothing."

Lily came home from school and Marcus sat with her in the kitchen while she drank a glass of milk. She asked why the phone was off the hook.

"Oh, there's a lot going on at work, I got tired of talking about it." He tried to sound nonchalant.

"Oh. Well, I have homework."

"Okay, why don't you do it now. Then maybe we'll make dinner together, surprise Pop."

"You're a terrible cook, Dad."

Good God, Marcus thought, *even my daughter hates my cooking.*

"I'm not that bad, am I?"

"Well," she said, getting up from the table and putting her glass in the dishwasher, "you do make good peanut butter and jelly sandwiches." She giggled on her way out of the kitchen.

Sass, Marcus thought. *We have a sassy daughter.*

Bob came home extra early, around 4:30.

"Why is the phone off the hook? I was worried."

"Oh, God. I'm sorry. I should have called you first." Marcus told him what had happened.

"Oh. Wow."

"Well, we better put it back on, I'm expecting to hear from Anna."

As soon as Marcus replaced it, it rang. It was the *San Diego Union-Tribune*, asking him for a comment on the arrest of Margaret Garner.

"No comment."

"Is it true, Sir, that you've been involved in investigating the murder?"

"No comment." He hung up.

It rang again. It was the *Los Angeles Times*. Same questions, same answers.

Bob started cooking and Anna called, and Bob told Marcus he could take it off the hook again.

They watched the local news at 6:00, and the arrest was the top story.

"This is going to be a shit-storm on campus," Marcus said.

"Pop, Dad said a bad word."

"I know honey, but he's had a really bad day. We won't punish him. This time."

After dinner, Jay showed up with a backpack and a surfboard. Lily hugged him and immediately wanted him to play gin rummy.

"Okay, but only two hands," he said.

"You're really taking up surfing?" Bob asked as Lily dealt the cards.

"Yeah, sure. Why not?"

"I mean, it's so . . ."

"So?"

"So Californian."

Everyone laughed.

60

Maggie Garner was arraigned first thing the next morning, and, the press reported, there was a fierce argument over bail. The prosecution, represented by First Assistant District Attorney Billy Lewis, asked that bail not be granted, based on "the heinous, cold-blooded nature of the crime," and pointed out that the defendant had the means to flee the country.

The judge granted bail at $5 million, with a bond of $500,000, and ordered Maggie to surrender her passport.

"Your Honor, the Mexican border is seventeen miles away. The defendant could leave the country without a passport," Lewis argued.

"I've made my ruling, counselor." A trial date was set for mid-June.

The press reported that George Garner was not in the courtroom.

Marcus silently thanked the Almighty that it was spring break and he didn't have to go to campus. The phone kept ringing for a while and then he kept it mostly off the hook. He took Zelda for an extra-long walk, hoping that would make him too tired to think about the case.

It didn't work. He tried to work out in his mind whether Maggie Garner could have hired someone to commit murder. Yes, she could be ruthless, and, at times, seemed heartless. She had to be, in her position, especially as a woman. The University was full of huge egos. It was a gigantic, complex institution with more federal dollars flowing through in research funds than almost any other campus in the country, thanks to the medical school, engineering, and oceanography.

But, he counter-argued to himself, jealousy can make people act irrationally. And, if her daughter was to be believed, Maggie no longer had a physical relationship with her husband, who everyone thought was a dullard.

He continued to turn it over and over in his head, and it was beginning to drive him crazy. He put the phone on the hook briefly and called Bob at his office, who turned out to be in court all day, Anna said. Anna could tell something was up, though, and suggested she meet Marcus for lunch. Marcus jumped at the chance to get out of the house and out of his head.

They met at a small bistro near Bob's office. After they ordered, Marcus started by saying how happy he and Bob both were that she turned down that job in LA and decided to stay.

"I'm glad too," she said. "It was a big firm and a lot of money but it just didn't feel like my kind of place. Too many straight, white male egos."

Marcus laughed.

"And," Anna said, "I couldn't leave Bob. He's family."

Marcus was genuinely touched. He smiled.

"The thing is, I know you guys have just weathered a bit of a storm," she said delicately.

"Yes, we have."

"He tells me almost everything. And, well, you know, he really felt awful about what happened. Still does. He was terrified he would lose you. I've never seen him in such a state."

"He's gone into therapy. And stopped drinking."

"Yes, I know. He gave me the bottle of scotch in his desk and told me to get rid of it."

"That's good. The thing is . . ."

Marcus paused, and Anna waited.

"The thing is, I'd be terrified of losing him too. I don't think I could stand it."

"I know it sounds corny, but sometimes, something like this brings a couple closer. I've seen it happen."

Marcus smiled.

"And I have news."

Marcus put down his coffee cup.

"I'm getting married."

"What?? When? Alejandro, of course." Alejandro was Anna's boyfriend, another lawyer, a corporate type. Both of them had come to dinner several times. He was an incredibly handsome, straightforward kind of guy, handsome enough to be in the movies, a Latin Gary Cooper.

"Yes. Alejandro. In June."

"That's wonderful. Congratulations! When he wasn't at Bob's birthday party, I wondered if you had broken up."

"No, no. He was out of town on a case. We've even bought a house. In Talmadge. We close in a couple of weeks."

Marcus was genuinely thrilled. "We'll throw you an engagement party!"

"Oh dios, no. Please. But kind of you to offer. It will be a very simple wedding."

"Well, we'll have you to an engagement dinner, how's that? Have you told Bob?"

"Just this morning. He was very happy, he started to cry. The other thing is . . . I'm pregnant."

"Oh my God!"

"How far along? How do you feel?"

"Two months. I feel fine, really. No morning sickness, nothing. No cravings. Nada."

"Do you have a good doctor?"

"Yes, very good. I'm fine, really. The only thing is, I can't stand the smell of fish, I don't know why."

"And Alejandro is . . .?"

"Over the moon. He has very little family. He's been singing to himself for weeks and watching me like I might expire at any minute."

"Well, let's celebrate. We'll order dessert."

Anna laughed and laughed. They ordered macaroons and coffee and, out on the sidewalk, hugged for a long time.

61

Later that afternoon, just as Lily was coming home from school, Jay and his friend Rick returned from surfing, leaving a few puddles on the floor. They hung their wetsuits out on the back patio and everyone sat around the kitchen table while Lily drank her milk and nibbled on an oatmeal cookie.

"These have no taste," she announced.

"Of course they don't," Marcus said. "They're good for you."

Rick was tall, muscular, blond, and soft-spoken, the epitome of polite California youth, with an easy, friendly manner. He made small talk with Lily and she invited him to play gin. He looked at Jay who quickly shook his head no, but Rick said, "Sure, we'll play."

While Lily ran to get the cards, Jay socked him in the arm.

"Ow. That hurt."

"She's a card shark. Beware."

They played on the kitchen table for a while, and then Marcus asked Lily if she had any homework.

"Yeah, okay, okay," she said, dejectedly.

Bob came home with several grocery bags and started cooking an elaborate Italian meal. Marcus made the salad.

"So, Anna," Marcus said.

"Yeah, isn't it great? I was wondering when it would happen. They seem really happy together, and they both seem thrilled about the baby. Alejandro keeps dropping in at the office to make sure she's okay and eating enough."

Marcus laughed.

"He's even talking about cutting back his hours at work while the baby is young."

"Can he do that?"

"Maybe. He just made partner. Of course this means Anna will need time off . . ."

"Small price to pay."

"Yeah. We've even been thinking of taking on another lawyer. You remember Laura, last year's clerk, from Yale? She's interested, after she finishes her clerkship with Judge Roth."

"She seemed really smart."

"Yes, she is. And we got along great. And she's so gorgeous, it will bring in business."

Marcus was surprised. "Does it really work that way?"

"Hello? Earth to Marcus. It's the real world out there. Full of straight men."

Marcus laughed.

Everyone enjoyed dinner, and then Jay and Rick did the dishes. After Lily went to bed, they said they wanted to talk. They settled around the dining room table with a pot of decaf.

"So, the thing is," Jay said, "we're together."

We figured," Bob said. Marcus nodded.

"So, should I tell Mom and Dad?" Jay asked.

"I came out to my parents a while back," Rick said, and smiled a dazzling smile.

"Well, if you feel like now is the right time," Bob said, "then yes."

"When did you tell Ruth and Jake?" Jay asked Bob.

"Oh, they knew. I made it official in high school."

"Really? Wow."

"Maybe they already have an inkling," Marcus said. "Parents often do. Especially if you haven't brought home a girlfriend by now."

"Right, right," Jay said, nervously. "I mean, Rick is the first guy I've . . . been with for more than a short time. And I've been with a few girls. But most guys our age, you know, they just want sex."

"I'm not like that. We just read poetry to each other," Rick said.

Everyone laughed.

"Should Rick be there when I tell them?" Jay asked.

Bob glanced at Marcus before answering. "Not the first conversation. But they should meet him, definitely."

"Okay. Will you guys be there when I tell them?" Jay asked, looking from Bob to Marcus.

"If you want us there, of course."

Jay looked relieved.

"Okay. Well, I think we'll go out for ice cream," Jay said. As they got up, he hugged Bob, and, to his surprise, Rick hugged both Bob and Marcus.

Rick whispered to Bob. "You're his hero, you know?"

After they left, Marcus chuckled. "Ah, young love."

"Maybe it will last," Bob said. "Maybe Jay's been lucky. Like me."

62

They went to bed happy, for Anna, for Jay. They got up early, as usual, to get Lily ready for school and take care of Zelda. Bob retrieved the newspapers from the front porch, the local paper and *The New York Times*. He started reading while Bob was in the shower.

"Oh, God," he said when Marcus sat down at the kitchen table. He sounded worried.

"What?"

Bob handed him *The San Diego Union-Tribune*.

There, starting on the front page, was a very long, detailed story about the affair between Maggie Garner and Chuck Silver, including excerpts from Chuck's diary, "obtained from a confidential source." The story included the information that Chuck also had an affair with Margaret Garner's daughter. And, the cherry on top, the reporter wrote, "UCSD professor Marcus George has been investigating the murder," without explaining why.

Marcus felt sick.

Lily could tell something was wrong. "What's the matter, Daddy?" she asked as she ate her cereal.

"Oh, nothing, sweet pea, just some silly stuff at work."

She left to catch the school bus, and Marcus turned to Bob.

"This is awful. It makes me sound like a busybody."

Bob frowned. "Maybe it would be a good idea to give an interview to a sympathetic reporter."

"Maybe. I'll ask Jason."

They both took turns reading and rereading the story.

"Who leaked all this, do you think?" Marcus asked.

"Well, it was either Emma or the police. Or the prosecution, to influence the jury pool. I'd put my money on the prosecution. I've seen it before," Bob said, with disgust in his voice.

As they passed the paper back and forth, Marcus kept feeling more and more sick to his stomach.

The excerpts from the diaries were lurid, detailing how "hot" Chuck found sex with both Maggie and Danielle, including the phrase "like mother, like daughter." The story included pictures of Maggie driving away from her house in sunglasses and Danielle, also wearing dark glasses, going to class at UCLA. There were quotes from "unnamed sources" about how many women Chuck bedded every month.

Officials at UCSD had no comment on the story, "except to remind everyone that any criminal defendant is innocent until proven guilty and deserves their day in court." Emma had been contacted as well, and she, too, had no comment. The story printed an old photo of her speaking somewhere, standing at a lectern.

"Remember," Bob said, putting his hand on Marcus's shoulder as he got ready to leave for work, "today's newspaper lines tomorrow's birdcage."

"Somehow I don't think this story will go away," Marcus said.

"No, it won't."

Shortly after Bob left, Jason rang the front doorbell.

"What a fucking mess," he said.

"Hello to you too."

"Sorry. But I mean, Jesus. Could they possibly have made it sound any more tawdry?"

"Well, you have to admit, it is tawdry. And tailor-made for splashy headlines."

"I guess so."

"Bob said maybe I should give an interview to someone, explain my role. There's nothing in the paper explaining why I'm involved."

"That's not a bad idea. Or Emma can put out a statement explaining your role. And mine. I'll call her."

The front doorbell rang again. Jason looked out the window in the living room. A television crew had pulled up and a reporter was standing at the door. He pulled down the blinds.

"Don't answer that. Close all the blinds, take the phone off the hook. I'll call Emma."

He dialed, explained what he thought Emma needed to say in a statement. She was reluctant, she said, but she'd speak to her attorney and call them back.

They sat at the kitchen table drinking coffee.

"I will have to leave the house sometime," Marcus said.

"Not today."

Emma called back quickly. Jason listened, took some notes, and thanked her.

"Her lawyer is going to put out a short statement explaining how we both got involved. But the press may still hound you. Say nothing."

After that, Marcus again took the phone off the hook.

Meanwhile, Jay finally got up.

"What's going on?" he asked, scratching his head. Marcus had all but forgotten he was in the house, and started to laugh, almost uncontrollably.

"You would probably sleep through an earthquake," Marcus said.

"I did once!" He got dressed, had some toast, and then sneaked out the back door. He climbed over the fence to meet Rick for another day's surfing.

By the time Lily got home from school, the press was gone from in front of the house, although the phone still rang every time Marcus put it back in the cradle..

63

The next morning, the *Union-Tribune* quoted a statement from Emma via her attorney, saying that she had asked "my colleague, Professor Marcus George, for a referral to a private investigator, which he kindly provided, and, at my request, helped the investigator whenever warranted." The story also identified Marcus as the person who had discovered Chuck's body.

"Well, that's a relief," Bob said.

Marcus looked unhappy. "It's a little vague. And I still hate being mixed up in this. I've hated it all along."

"I know. But vague is good in these things."

That morning's story contained more lurid excerpts from Chuck's diary: excerpts about other women, including some passages bordering on the pornographic. The story referred to Chuck as "a sex addict leading a double life," which, now that Marcus thought about it, might really be true. Except if his wife was aware of what he was doing, could it really be called a double life? He wasn't sure, and thinking about it gave him a headache.

Jason was becoming more and more certain that the source of the press stories was the DA's office, hoping to influence the jury pool.

"They overdid it, though," Jason said over the phone. "There's been so much press, Maggie's attorney will ask for a change of venue, and she might actually get it."

Bob, who had briefly worked for the DA's office, agreed that was the most likely explanation for the leaks.

They spent a quiet weekend at home. Jay and Rick came to dinner on Saturday, and on Sunday took Lily to the zoo. While at home they played round after round of gin and Monopoly, Lily winning every time.

"She has powers," Jay said at one point. "Beware."

Finally it was Monday morning. Break was over and Marcus had to go back to campus, which he dreaded.

He dressed carefully. Bob wished him luck. Jason asked if he wanted him to go with him; he declined, reasoning that Jason would look like a bodyguard and just create more of a ruckus. Once at the campus, he parked and took the elevator up to his floor. Mercifully, he passed few people in the hall.

His office phone rang as he was preparing his class. It was the Chancellor's office, summoning Marcus to a meeting that afternoon at 3:00.

"Shit," he murmured out loud as he hung up the phone.

For a few minutes he stood staring out the window, finally

pulling himself together with a sigh. He needed to get back to work. It was the first day of the Spring quarter, and, as luck would have it, he was teaching a new course called "American Radicalism." He had wanted to teach it for years, and his program finally agreed. It had enrolled 120 students, which meant Marcus would have to lecture, but at the moment he dreaded it. The first time through a new lecture course was always a huge amount of work.

The class met at 11:00 in one of the large lecture halls on the ground floor of his building. He had asked his two graduate student assistants to meet him at 10:00 to go over things, and they arrived promptly. After getting business out of the way, he brought up the elephant in the room.

"Do you want to ask me anything about recent events?"

The two students, one male, one female, looked at each other.

"Um," one of them said haltingly, "do you think Margaret Garner is guilty of murder?"

Marcus was relieved; the question wasn't about him.

"I have no idea, really. I think we have to let the legal process play itself out."

They both nodded.

They gathered their things and went down to the lecture hall. In the elevator they ran into two colleagues from another department, who raised their eyebrows but said nothing.

The lecture hall was packed, and Marcus took the stage. Professor George was on.

64

The lecture went well, and he fielded the usual questions about course requirements and exams.

It was almost noon when the lecture ended, and Marcus

realized he was hungry. He also realized he should have packed a lunch to avoid the faculty club, or any cafeteria on campus, but had been too nervous that morning to think of such a mundane thing. As he left the lecture hall, Jim Stewart was waiting for him outside.

"Jim, my God."

"Hey. I had a feeling you'd need a friendly lunch partner."

Jim, retired, had an office on campus but seldom appeared. Marcus breathed deeply, then said, "Oh, God. You have no idea how right you are."

"Arlene's in the car, we can take you off campus, then drop you back," Jim said.

Marcus thought for a moment. "No, I don't want to hide. Let's get Arlene and go to the faculty club."

"Really? Are you sure?"

"Yes. With you two there, what could happen?"

"Well," Jim said, chuckling, "I can think of a few things, but it's up to you."

"Let's do it."

Arlene was idling at the curb with the motor running. Jim leaned in to her window.

"He doesn't want a clean getaway. We're going to the faculty club."

"Ah." Arlene smiled, found a parking spot, and the three of them walked over.

Marcus hesitated a bit as they entered.

"Courage," Jim said.

They walked into the main dining room, which was filling up, and snagged a table at the side, near a window. There were lots of glances their way, along with that perfectly obvious attempt of people to hide the fact that they were staring. It reminded Marcus of a similar experience at the Harvard faculty club, decades earlier. He smiled at the memory. Nothing really changes in academia, he thought; people just get older. And in California, a bit less polite.

They took their seats and then made their way to the buffet table. More stares. Several people sidled over to greet Jim and Arlene; they all ignored Marcus, which was fine with him. Finally, plates filled, they sat down to eat.

"Thank God you're here," Marcus said.

"Oh, we wouldn't have missed this for the world. All these people wondering what we're talking about. We haven't had this much fun since we were invited to the White House."

"When were you at the White House? And why? I mean, how did . . . "

"Our son. He works at Treasury. He got us tickets for the special tour, the one most tourists don't get, and we ran into Laura Bush."

"She was lovely," Arlene added. "Too bad she's married to a war criminal."

Marcus chuckled.

"So . . ." Jim finally asked. "What should we think about Maggie?"

"Honestly, I have no idea. I don't know what evidence the police found. It appears to be true that she didn't want the affair to end, but that was years ago."

"And the daughter? Have you met her?"

"Yes. The phrase that comes to mind is 'a piece of work.'"

"Could Maggie have been driven over the edge by the affair with the daughter?" Arlene asked. It was the obvious question.

"Maggie's not the type to go over the edge," Jim said. Marcus nodded.

"Should we brave the dessert table?" Arlene asked.

"Why not?" Marcus said. He was feeling supported and brave, at least for the moment.

At the dessert table, he turned around and faced Rudd Martin.

I should have known he'd be here today, he thought to himself. "Rudd."

"Marcus. How awful this must be for you. And for poor Emma."

"I'm just a bystander, really. I'm fine. Have you talked to Emma?"

"Briefly. She's upset. Of course."

"Yes, of course. It would be strange if she weren't."

He left it at that, smiled at Rudd, and carried his cookies back to the table.

They lingered over coffee, and a few more people came up to say hello to Jim and Arlene. Finally they got up and walked to the parking lot.

"I don't know how to thank you," Marcus said. "You are saints. I owe you, big time."

"Nonsense," Jim said. Arlene kissed his cheek. Marcus watched them walk to their car.

65

Marcus called Bob at his office and told him what had happened so far—the summons to the Chancellor, lunch.

"The Chancellor. Eesh. What do you think he'll say?"

"I have no idea."

"Well, if you need a good lawyer, I know someone. We can barter for my services."

"Very funny. Can you call Cathy, ask her to meet Lily when she gets home?"

"Yes of course."

"See you later. If I'm not rotting in a cell in the basement of some abandoned university building."

Bob laughed.

It was 1:00. Marcus did his best to concentrate on writing his next lecture, on Tom Paine, the original American radical, and it went fairly well. He kept staring out the window at the choppy Pacific.

At 2:45 he gathered his things and made his way to the Chancellor's office, his stomach churning.

He had met the Chancellor, Frank Atkins, a physicist by training, only once, at a welcoming party when Atkins first arrived. He struck Marcus as a smooth operator. He had heard him speak at various meetings, of course, and thought he had that rare gift of being able to sound intelligent while saying absolutely nothing of substance. He had risen quickly through the UCSD ranks; too quickly, many thought. Everyone assumed that sooner or later he would land in the UC President's office in Oakland, if not in Sacramento or Washington.

Marcus announced himself to one of the secretaries and took a seat. At 3:10, another secretary came and fetched him and brought him into the Chancellor's inner office.

"Marcus," the Chancellor said, getting up from his large desk. "Is it all right if I call you Marcus?"

The Chancellor offered his hand. Marcus shook it. "Of course."

Atkins pointed to two comfortable chairs. The secretary asked Marcus if he wanted anything to drink, and he said a cup of coffee would be lovely. She fetched it.

While waiting for it, Marcus noticed the Chancellor's hand-crafted suit. He estimated it cost at least $3,000.

The coffee arrived and the secretary departed, closing the door behind her.

"So, Marcus, tell me how you got mixed up in this mess."

Marcus took a sip of coffee, and noticed it was better than the coffee anywhere else on campus. He decided to be straightforward.

"Actually, Maggie dragged me into it."

The Chancellor looked genuinely surprised. He waited. Marcus took another sip of coffee. He found himself wishing it were scotch.

"After Chuck was found and the investigation was underway, Emma was questioned by the police. That rattled her. She wanted to talk to an attorney, and she knew my partner, Bob Abramson, practices criminal law, and that he's tried murder cases. Maggie called me at home to ask us—both of us—to meet with Emma. So we did. Reluctantly. But I didn't think we could say no."

"I see. And then?"

"And then, Emma said she wanted to hire an investigator. She didn't entirely trust that the police would do a good job. It's still not clear that they have. So Bob recommended Jason Thompson, who's a former San Diego police detective. He later worked as Bob's investigator for many years—and he's a friend of ours."

"Well, all that makes sense, but what explains your continuing role?"

"Jason has very little experience with our world. He needed to question a large number of academics, both here in town and around the country, in New York, Chicago, Detroit, in the . . . He wanted me there as someone who knew how all of us operate, what's typical and what's not."

"Well, Marcus, that may be where you made your mistake."

"In retrospect, that may well be true, sir. But I wanted to help Emma find her husband's killer. Certainly you can understand that. And there was no way to know Maggie would end up a suspect, much less being charged. Or that Chuck's intimate journal would be leaked to the press."

"True." Atkins shifted in his chair.

Marcus waited. Finally, he asked whether he had violated any University rules or policies.

"No, no. That's not what this is about. But I wonder if you could step back now. The press is eating us alive. The fewer UCSD personnel involved in the case, the better. This whole mess is a PR disaster. It could have repercussions for years."

"Well, at this point, it seems the legal process will take over."

"Yes, that looks to be the case."

There was an awkward silence.

"Was there anything else, Sir?"

"No. I just wanted to chat. Thanks for coming in."

And with that, the Chancellor went back to his desk. It was clear he was not going to give Marcus another thought.

66

As he left the administrative complex, Marcus felt more stares coming his way from the staff, who worked in a large, open space. He smiled.

He went back to his office, collected his things, and drove home. He couldn't decide if he was pissed off or pleased to have stood up for himself. Probably both, he decided.

When he got home, Lily and Cathy were playing cards, and he heard Lily yell out "GIN" as he walked into the kitchen. Zelda came out to greet him.

"Whatever you do," he said to Cathy, "don't play for money. She'll clean you out."

Lily giggled, and Cathy hugged her good-bye.

"Pop called," Lily said. "He said he'd stop at the Greek place and pick up dinner."

"Well that's good, you like Greek food, don't you?"

"Yeah, except those funny green things."

"You mean the grape leaves? Why don't you like them?"

"They're slimy. Yuck."

Marcus laughed. "Homework?"

"Yeah, okay. When will you guys stop asking me about homework?"

"When you graduate from an Ivy League college."

Lily thought that was hilarious. "I'm going to Berkeley," she announced, and Marcus stared after her as she went to her room. Eleven years old and she knows where she wants to go to college.

The next day, Marcus and Bob had another appointment with David Drake, the therapist. They settled into his office at 8:00 after getting Lily off to school.

"So, who wants to start?"

"I do," Marcus said, surprising both Bob and Drake.

Marcus took a moment to gather his thoughts.

"When I was in New York recently with Jason on business—he's also a friend of ours—we went to a couple of gay bars. And I bumped into a former student."

"And?" Drake asked.

"Well, he was my student many years ago, when I first started teaching, as an assistant professor. So we're actually pretty close in age. I'm now almost fifty, he's maybe in his early forties."

Bob looked apprehensive. Marcus went on.

"So we chatted, and he told me that he had always had a crush on me. I was completely surprised. He was drinking and I think that was mostly the liquor talking. He sort of propositioned me. And I was flattered, I admit." He paused. "I felt . . . tempted."

"And?" Drake asked.

They must teach that word a lot in therapist school, Marcus said to himself.

"I thanked him and turned him down."

Bob let out a sigh of relief.

"But the thing is," Marcus said, looking down, "I was kind

of aroused."

"Aroused how?" Drake asked.

"Physically."

"That's only natural," Drake said. "An attractive man had just propositioned you."

"The thing is, if I had been in a different state of mind, I can imagine I could have gone home with him. If I had been depressed or upset." He looked over at Bob. "If I were going through a difficult time."

"And?"

That word again, Marcus thought.

"And so I had a better understanding of what Bob did. His father had just died. Suddenly. No warning. This blond hunk appeared suddenly in Bob's life and . . . and Bob slipped. I get it. In a way I hadn't before."

"It doesn't make it okay," Bob said quietly, looking down.

"Maybe not. But I understand it on a level I didn't before."

"Would it have been so terrible to go home with that former student? To have a fling?" Drake asked.

"Terrible, no. But it would have been revenge." He paused. "That's not me."

"So are you saying you want your relationship with Bob to be monogamous? That's unusual, after so many years, among gay couples."

"I do want that. And maybe it is unusual, or maybe I'm weird. Honestly, I don't really care. But . . ."

"But?"

"It's up to Bob."

Marcus knew this was one of his life's crucial moments. He held his breath.

"I'm fine with it. Really." Bob said simply.

"Good. And have you forgiven Bob, would you say, Marcus?"

Drake asked. They both looked at him.

"I'm getting there. I mean admit I was hurt. Still am, a little. But I'm getting there. So . . ."

"So?"

"So let's see how it goes. How we do."

"I can live with that," Bob said. He smiled.

Ever the professor, Marcus wondered if the relief he felt was akin to Lincoln realizing the North was about to win the Civil War.

67

That afternoon, Jason and Marcus met for lunch in Hillcrest. Jason had spoken to Detective Sanchez, off the record, and had some information about the prosecution's case against Maggie Garner.

"I'm not sure I need to hear this, or that I should," Marcus said. He told Jason about being called on the carpet by the Chancellor.

"Screw him," Jason said. "You haven't done anything wrong. Have you violated any campus rules?"

"I asked him that. He admitted I hadn't."

"Look. You were asked by your boss, Maggie, to help out a colleague. Emma. What were you supposed to do? Ignore it?"

"I know. But I don't think I've gained any fans at my place of employment."

"Does that matter? Don't you have tenure?"

"Yes, they can't really do anything to me, it's true. But . . ."

"But?"

Marcus thought for a moment. "The coin of the realm at a place like UCSD is reputation. Mine has taken a hit."

"It won't be permanent, I bet."

"Maybe not. And there's nothing I can do about it now."

Their food arrived.

"Do you want me to talk to him? I can confirm your story."

Marcus smiled. "Thanks, no. I don't think that would help."

"Okay. So do you want to hear about Maggie?"

"Why not? In for a penny, in for a pound." It was an old expression of Marcus's mother. He hadn't thought of it in years.

"Okay. So. This is all top-secret, of course. The police found large withdrawals from financial accounts. Definitely made by Maggie, not her husband. He didn't know about them. And Maggie was spotted by eyewitnesses in a shady neighborhood in Los Angeles. She stood out like a sore thumb, in her power suit and high heels."

"Wow."

"And she was seen near the home of a known hitman for organized crime."

"Oh my God. So they think . . ."

"They think the cash was used to pay for a hit on Chuck Silver."

Marcus put down his fork. "Has the hitman turned on her?"

"That's the thing I can't figure out. He's disappeared. So they don't have the shooter, or the gun, and everything is circumstantial. It's not a strong case. Although she'll have to explain what she was doing in that part of LA."

"Well, the case against Isaacson wasn't strong either. That didn't stop them."

"God knows what's going on in the DA's office. Rumor is, total chaos."

"She has a good lawyer, right?"

"Definitely. I wouldn't want to be the DA right now."

For a moment they were quiet.

"So how are things at home?" Jason finally asked.

"Better."

"Good. I couldn't stand it if you two broke up."

Marcus was touched. He never thought of Jason as the sentimental type.

"Listen," he said, "Anna is getting married."

"Oh! That lawyer, right? What's his name?"

"Yeah. Alejandro. He of the expensive suits."

Jason laughed.

We're having them to dinner this weekend. Saturday. Why don't you come?"

"Sure. Love to. Can I bring the historian?"

Marcus was surprised. "Sure. So that's going well?"

"Yeah. I like him. A lot. Even though he reads too much."

Marcus couldn't stop laughing at that.

68

They decided to go all out at the dinner for Anna and Alejandro. Bob left work early Friday to shop for his favorite recipes out of Julia Child, including beef bourguignon. He loved to cook elaborate meals and seldom had the time. Marcus and Lily made decorations, streamers and a banner saying "Congratulations!" Marcus went to the liquor store on Saturday morning to buy the best Pinot Noir he could find.

Lily was especially excited. She loved Anna, who had spent so much time working with Bob and had even baby-sat for her a few times. And she liked helping Bob out in the kitchen. When it was time to get ready, she put on her best dress.

They were so busy with the dinner that they didn't have time to read the paper that morning, which carried a story on one of the inside pages that said that Margaret Garner's attorney was flooding the court with pre-trial motions.

Jason arrived with Joel Sanders and two bottles of very good champagne. Soon after, Anna and Alejandro arrived, Anna looking radiant in a red dress. Lily hugged her.

"Anna, you feel different!" Lily said.

Anna looked over at Bob and Marcus with an expression that said, "should I tell her?" And Bob said, "why not?"

Anna took Lily's hand. "Well, sweetheart, I feel different because I'm going to have a baby!"

Alejandro beamed and put his arms around Anna's shoulders.

For a moment Lily looked confused, and then she burst into a big smile. "Oh! That's so nice! I'll baby-sit!"

Jason hugged her and kissed her on both cheeks and shook Alejandro's hand.

Marcus opened one bottle of champagne. Bob, newly abstemious, and Anna, pregnant, both abstained, but everyone else was glad to raise a toast.

"Do you know if it's a boy or a girl?" Lily asked.

"Actually, we just found out. It's a boy!"

"What's his name?" Lily asked. She was excited.

Anna laughed. "Well, probably Alejandro. Like his father."

They sat down to dinner. Everyone loved the food. Anna and Alejandro talked about their new house.

After Lily went reluctantly to bed, they settled in the living room with coffee. Joel Sanders brought up Maggie Garner.

"Marcus, how did you get involved? The case is all anyone talks about on campus these days."

"I know," Marcus said. He tried to sound nonchalant.

"Word is, you got called on the carpet by the Chancellor."

"Good grief," Marcus said. "There really are no secrets in academia, are there?"

"This is my fault," Jason said. He told a brief version of how they both got involved in the case, and Marcus gave a short version of his meeting with the Chancellor.

"Interesting," Sanders said. "You know . . . maybe I shouldn't say this . . . but I know Emma. We were on a committee together, one that met over two years. And I got the feeling she was coming on to me."

Jason glanced at Marcus. Both looked really surprised.

"Really?" Jason said.

"Yes. Several times. It got uncomfortable, to tell the truth. I was untenured at the time."

Marcus could tell Jason was thinking.

"Do you think Garner is guilty?" Alejandro asked.

"Honestly, I don't know," Marcus said. Jason nodded.

"The DA's case seems awfully circumstantial, at least based on what's been reported so far in the press," Bob said.

"Yes, that's true," Alejandro said. "My firm had some dealings with her husband, George."

"Oh?" Jason's curiosity was aroused.

"Yes. Strange guy. But then most accountants are. He was in our offices last week. I had some work to do with him—he does our books, and I was involved in a complex settlement case, we had to go through a lot of documents."

"And?" Jason asked.

"Well, I tried to offer sympathy about his family's trouble, but he brushed it off. I got the feeling that he found the whole thing funny. At one point he started to laugh. It was very odd."

Jason glanced at Marcus again.

Anna could see talking about the case was making people somber and a little uncomfortable, so she changed the subject.

"We've been planning the wedding. It will be small, at church, we don't want a big fuss. But we were thinking, we'd really like Lily to be the flower girl."

"Oh!" Bob said. "That's lovely. She'll love that!"

After everyone left, as they were cleaning up, Bob asked Marcus about Jason and Joel Sanders.

"What's with Jason? I mean, this is so out of character for him. A professor?"

"I know. But they seemed really at ease, didn't they? And he seems like a nice guy."

"Yeah, he does. But can it last? Is it just another fling for Jason?"

Marcus thought for a moment. "Maybe he's tired of flings. And what they say about opposites attracting . . ."

"Yes. Interesting, what Joel said about Emma," Bob said.

"Yeah. Very."

"He doesn't strike me as the type that would make something like that up, or read too much into things."

"No," Marcus responded. "He doesn't."

69

Campus gossip seemed to die down over the next few weeks, to Marcus's great relief. He was busy with lectures for his course, and Bob and Anna were involved in the usual run of cases.

They took Lily to visit the Mission Hills Academy, which she loved. The school gave her a battery of tests on a Saturday, after which she met with a panel of teachers. On the following Monday the school principal called to confirm that Lily was, in fact, intellectually gifted for her age, and said they would be happy to have her enroll in the Fall.

She was thrilled, as were both Bob and Marcus.

"Now you know, sweet pea, this will mean you'll have to work harder than you do now."

"Good," was her only reply.

Emma pushed Jason to continue investigating Chuck's murder,

but he resisted; he said they should wait to see if Maggie Garner was found guilty. She wasn't happy with that but eventually agreed.

Emma reappeared on campus. She wasn't teaching but spent the occasional afternoon in her office, and was even seen having lunch with one or two colleagues at the faculty club, including the Steins. She dressed in black whenever she appeared, which Marcus thought was overdoing it a bit, and he noticed that she didn't look particularly well.

Then, one Thursday morning in late April, Marcus and Bob awoke to a front-page story saying that the court was to hold a hearing on Maggie Garner's motion to have her case dismissed. The story was short on details, but said a hearing was scheduled for that afternoon.

Jason called and said he would attend the hearing. Marcus asked him if he knew what was going on.

"No idea."

It turned out to be a media zoo, with cameras and crowds outside the courthouse. Maggie and her attorneys were stone-faced as they made their way through the crowds outside and in the hallways. The courtroom itself was jammed and Jason could only find a seat by squeezing into the last row of benches.

The judge entered and the hearing began.

"Counselor, please proceed."

Maggie's attorney, Darren Jacobs, was the epitome of a sophisticated lawyer, with an expensive suit, expensive haircut, a voice that might persuade the Almighty himself.

The argument was both technical and volatile. It boiled down to the claim that the search warrant used to search the Garner home was defective.

"The police officer who obtained the warrant did not swear under oath that the information he received about the presence of a gun in the Garner home came from a reliable source. As such, the search was a clear violation of the Fourth Amendment."

Much murmuring in the courtroom. The judge banged his gavel.

"Do you have any evidence of this?" the judge asked.

"Yes, your honor. We call Detective Douglas Mulroney to the stand."

Mulroney rose, took the stand, and was sworn in. He looked both nervous and defiant.

"Detective Mulroney, you were assigned to investigate the murder of Charles Silver, which took place on December 27 of last year, is that correct?"

"Yes."

"And, in the course of your investigation, did you obtain information you claimed was reliable about the presence of a gun in the Garner home?"

He tried to look calm but it wasn't working. "Yes."

"On the basis of that information, you obtained a warrant for a search of the Garner home in La Jolla from Judge Abraham, did you not?"

"Yes."

Jacobs paused, dramatically.

"Did you produce a written statement about this information, and swear under oath that the information came from a reliable source?"

Mulroney looked at the judge, who looked at him sternly.

"Detective?" Jacobs repeated.

"Answer the question, Detective Mulroney," the judge said.

The witness started to sweat. "No, I did not."

"In fact, Detective, you considered the informant's tip unreliable, is that not correct?"

Mulroney paused and started to sweat. "I wasn't sure."

"And why was that, detective?"

Mulroney turned bright red. "Because the informant's information had proven wrong in the past."

The gallery erupted and the judge banged his gavel and threatened to clear the courtroom.

Maggie smiled ever so slightly.

"As such, your honor," Jacobs went on, "this search was a clear violation of my client's constitutional rights. Every piece of evidence that was subsequently collected, including her financial records, followed from that search, and, as such, according to well-established precedent, were fruit of the poisonous tree."

The judge looked disgusted. He paused. The courtroom was silent.

"I agree, with great reluctance. All such evidence is excluded."

"We move for an immediate dismissal," Jacobs said, returning to his table. "The state has no case."

Billy Lewis, the ADA, rose and spoke for the first time.

"Your honor, the people object."

"Oh, I'm sure you do, Mr. Lewis."

The judge was clearly weighing what to do. The tension in the room was palpable. Moments passed.

"Motion granted. The defendant is free to go. Charges are dismissed, without prejudice. Detective, report to your superiors."

The judge banged his gavel and quickly left the bench.

"Sheesh," the older reporter sitting next to Jason said, "that was like a Perry Mason episode."

Outside the courthouse, Jacobs and Maggie stood in front of makeshift microphones that had been set up.

Jacobs was terse. "We are gratified that justice has been done. The San Diego police department needs to clean house. This never should have happened."

He said no more, and he and Maggie quickly ducked into a

waiting limo.

Jason watched the scene outside the courthouse and then went to meet Marcus at home.

"How the hell could the police have messed up like that? And how did the defense find out?" Marcus was pacing.

"I don't know. But someone in the department knew what happened and went to Jacobs. I'd bet on it. It might even have been Sanchez."

"Of course," Jason added, "this doesn't mean she didn't do it."

"No. It doesn't."

70

Emma called Jason that afternoon and wanted to meet with him and with Marcus again. Marcus said he needed to pull back, so Jason went alone.

Emma appeared to be slightly drunk. She had a glass of scotch in her hand. She wanted to continue the investigation, but Jason convinced her that, at this point, she was wasting her money and he was wasting his time. The trail was cold and all the suspects had alibis.

"Not every crime gets solved," he told her, "and this may be one of them. Also, you never know, the police may still find something. Or find more evidence against Maggie Garner, charge her again. It's possible. The judge left open that possibility."

Emma reluctantly agreed to let things go. "For now," she said.

Maggie remained in seclusion, and a story appeared in the press that she and George had legally separated. The campus administration said nothing about whether Maggie could return to her administrative position, which, for a while, was what everyone gossiped about on campus.

Jay and Rick came to dinner several times, and Lily seemed to bond strongly with Rick, who played cards with her whenever she asked. At one dinner in May, Jay said he was ready to talk to his parents; he and asked Marcus and Bob to join him in LA the following weekend.

They drove up on a Saturday, picking up Ruth on the way. Ruth and Jay sat in the back seat with Lily and took turns tickling her.

That night Bob and Ruth did the cooking, gabbing way. Everyone seemed in a good mood.

After Lily and Ruthie had gone to bed, Jay looked at his parents and said he had something to tell them. Ruth was passing around cups of coffee.

"The thing is," he said, "I've been seeing someone. At school."

"That's great," Carol said. Alex nodded.

"Um, the thing is, the person I'm seeing is a guy. I'm gay. Or maybe bi. But mostly gay, I think."

"We know," Alex said, nodding.

"You know??" Jay was incredulous.

"We didn't know for sure," Carol said, "we just had a feeling. A pretty strong feeling."

"For how long?" Jay seemed completely taken aback.

"Oh, for a while," Alex said. "I mean, there's never been a girl in the picture, we just kinda assumed."

"Parents pick up on these things," Ruth said, smiling. "At least, some do."

"So it's okay? You don't mind?"

"Of course it's okay," Carol said. Alex nodded again. "Earth to Jay. This is 2004. LA. Not 1950 Oklahoma."

Jay started laughing and shaking his head. "I was so worried."

"So tell us about this young man," Alex said.

Jay told them about Rick, how they met, how they both were

thinking about medical school, and he told them about surfing. He said he'd bring Rick home to meet them soon.

"Just don't forget," Ruth said, "I still want great-grandchildren. One way or another."

"I promise, Gran," Jay said, looking over at Bob and Marcus.

"Now," Ruth said, "let's have dessert."

The following Monday, on the 50th anniversary of Brown v. Board of Education, the highest court in Massachusetts legalized gay marriage.

71

Memorial Day weekend came, and Jay and Rick invited Marcus and Bob and Lily to come to Tourmaline for a picnic and to watch them surf, which Lily had been wanting to do for weeks.

"We'll take care of the food," Jay said, "Rick is good at all that kitchen stuff."

They went on Monday. It was hazy but pleasantly warm, the beginning of the annual period known as June Gloom, when the city, and especially the beaches, were covered in clouds and mist.

They parked on La Jolla Boulevard and hiked the short distance to the beach. Jay and Rick carried a cooler and then went back to the car for their surfboards while Bob and Marcus and Lily found a spot on the beach. The boys did the San Diego shuffle, changing into their wetsuits by holding a towel around each other for modesty's sake.

The waves were "only" medium, Rick announced, but still, there was occasionally enough swell to surf. Lily went up to the edge of the water to watch them; they swam out and waited for the next big wave, then glided effortlessly to shore.

Lily clapped and jumped up and down. After another wave, they all joined Bob and Marcus on the quilt.

"It looks easy," Lily said.

Jay laughed. "It's not. Believe me. It's really hard to keep your balance. It takes a lot of practice."

"I bet I could do it," Lily said.

"No," Bob and Marcus said in unison. Lily gave them a dirty look.

"I brought something for you," Rick quickly said to Lily, and he pulled a deck of cards out of the cooler. Lily squealed and they played several hands of gin.

They ate the sandwiches Rick had made, turkey and ham, with fruit for dessert. After resting for a while, Rick and Jay rode several more waves. Both Bob and Marcus dozed, and both felt completely relaxed for the first time in a long time.

Around 3:00, they packed up and started walking back to the car down Tourmaline Street. They were planning to have a barbecue at home that evening and had invited Jason and Joel to join them.

And, as they walked, Marcus saw, across the street and down the block, a man wearing a flowing scarf emerge from one of the buildings and get into a car. He was wearing a hat to hide his face.

72

I need to make a phone call," Marcus said as they got into the car.

"Now?" Bob asked.

"Yeah."

They drove to a nearby gas station and Marcus got out and used the pay phone. He dialed Jason's home number. Joel Sanders answered and put Jason on the line.

"Which building at Tourmaline did Chuck have an apartment in?" Marcus asked.

Jason told him, and Marcus said, "What apartment number?"

When they hung up, Marcus went back to the car and said they needed to go back to the beach for a minute, he needed to do something. Everyone was puzzled but Bob drove back, wondering what on earth was going on.

"Stop here," Marcus said, in front of the building. Everyone looked at him like he was crazy.

He got out and took the elevator up to the third floor. He knocked on the door of apartment 306.

After a moment, Emma opened the door. She was wearing a nightgown and open robe.

"Well, hello," she said, with a strange smile. She was holding a glass of liquor. Marcus turned around and left.

He said nothing.

He felt slightly dizzy as he walked back to the car, then forced himself to smile as he got in.

"My mistake. I thought I saw an old friend."

73

When they got home, Marcus went into the bedroom and called Jason, who came over right away with Joel. Jason and Marcus promptly disappeared into Marcus's study.

"What's going on?" Joel asked Bob out in the living room. "I feel like I just stepped into a James Bond movie."

"I have no idea," Bob said, staring at the closed door to Marcus's study.

When Jason and Marcus emerged, both looking grim, they

announced that they needed to run an errand.

"If we're not back by dinnertime, go ahead without us."

"What's happening?" Bob asked, alarmed.

"We'll explain later," Marcus said on his way out the door.

They got into Jason's car. Bob and Joel, astonished, stared after them as they drove away.

"We'll go to La Jolla. She'll have gone home by now," Jason said.

They sped to Emma's house and rang the doorbell. The maid opened the door and said that Ms. Baker was "not at home."

"Yes, she is," Jason said, and pushed past the maid. Marcus followed. He felt like he was crossing some invisible line he had never crossed.

Emma was standing at the far end of the living room, drinking from a crystal glass. They could smell scotch. She had a half-smile.

"Gentlemen," she said.

"You told us you had never visited Chuck's apartment," Jason said.

She smiled. "Yes, I did say that."

"And," Marcus said, "you've been using it to have an affair with Rudd Martin."

Emma sat down on one of the couches and took another sip. She carefully adjusted her slacks and the gold chain around her neck. She was moving in slow motion.

"What of it?"

"This means that both you and he had a motive to kill your husband," Jason said, struggling to keep his voice even. He and Marcus continued to stand, facing her.

"Come now. I hired you to find the killer."

"You could have done that to throw suspicion elsewhere. Deflection. It's been known to happen."

She scoffed. "That's absurd."

They waited, but Emma said nothing else for a long while. She got up and walked over to the glass doors leading to the patio and stared at the pool. She drank more of her scotch.

Finally, she spoke again, very slowly, still looking out the window.

"I ignored his other life. For a long time. And I probably would have gone on ignoring it. We were happy. In our own way."

"What changed?" Jason asked.

Emma turned toward them.

"He gave me HIV. That's what changed."

Jason and Marcus looked at each other. Marcus turned red and Jason let out a long breath.

"And?" Jason asked.

"And that ended . . ."

"Ended what?" Marcus could see Jason's patience was gone. He was getting angrier by the minute.

"That ended our intimate life."

"I'm sorry to hear all this," Jason said after a long pause. "Very sorry. But that doesn't justify murder. You're going to need a very good lawyer."

"Don't be ridiculous. I didn't want Charles dead. I would never have done that to Chloe. She loves her father. Loved. Needed him."

"And Rudd? After all, you're going to be a very wealthy woman."

Emma looked genuinely shocked. The color drained from her face. After a moment she walked back to the center of the room and steadied herself by grabbing the back of a chair with one hand. Marcus could see she was struggling to regain her composure.

"I can't believe Rudd would do this." There was a slight tremor in her voice. "But if he did, it was his decision. I had nothing to do with it." She drained her glass, her hand shaking slightly.

"The police may see it differently," Jason said, ice in his voice.

"You can't go to the police. I hired you. You work for me."

"Our relationship is not privileged. And even if it were, there is something called the crime-fraud exception. You might want to look it up. And you have no hold on Marcus."

Marcus looked away.

Emma sat down again on one of the couches. They waited for her to speak.

"Rudd wouldn't do this. I know nothing about who killed Charles."

"If that's your story, lady, you better stick to it."

Jason turned around. Marcus followed him out the door.

As they left, they heard the crystal glass smash against a wall.

74

They got back to the barbecue just as everyone was finishing. There was lots of food left over, and Marcus and Jason ate without much appetite.

"Where were you, Daddy?" Lily asked Marcus.

"Oh, just a silly work thing, nothing to worry about."

Marcus smiled. How he wished that were true. He realized he would now be called to testify.

As they undressed for bed, Marcus told Bob what had happened.

"I had a feeling it was something like that," Bob replied, putting his hand on Marcus's shoulder.

The next morning, early, Jason and Marcus met and together went to police headquarters. They spoke to Detective Sanchez.

"We suspected all along," Sanchez said. "But we had no proof."

Warrants were obtained, legally this time, for searches

of Emma's home and office and Rudd Martin's, as well as the apartment at the beach.

The police found a gun in Rudd Martin's kitchen. Ballistics tests quickly proved it was the murder weapon. No other physical evidence was discovered.

Rudd was promptly charged with first-degree murder.

In stories in the press, Rudd, through his lawyer, strongly hinted that he was driven to the murder by Emma Baker.

Emma hired Sidney Carter, a famous and high-priced Los Angeles defense attorney. Through him, she maintained that she had no involvement in the murder and was "shocked" to discover that her lover had killed her husband. The police said they were sure they had apprehended the murderer and that they had no comment about "other parties," but that the investigation was ongoing.

For a while the press badgered Marcus, but that died down quickly.

75

A story appeared in the press about Maggie Garner. She was not going to go back to serving as Vice Chancellor but would resume her role as Professor of Anthropology. She and George were quietly divorced and Maggie moved to a smaller house. The rumor was that Maggie had extricated her daughter Danielle from a drug house in Los Angeles and that that's what she was doing in that shady neighborhood. The cash withdrawal was to pay her drug debts.

"Do you believe it?" Bob asked Marcus.

"Who knows?"

By this time, Marcus wanted to forget about everything

connected to the case. In fact, he wanted to forget most of the previous year.

"I wonder . . ." Bob started to say.

"Hmm?"

"I wonder if Danielle gave Chuck HIV. If she was using hard drugs . . ."

"You're right," Marcus said, dumbstruck. "That could explain it."

Rudd Martin was placed on administrative leave at UCSD. His trial date was set for September. Emma took a voluntary leave of absence.

76

Anna and Alejandro's wedding day approached. Anna took Lily shopping for a dress she could wear as flower girl. Bob went with them and they bought her a very grown-up looking pale pink dress, which Lily loved, and new shoes to match.

The traditional Catholic ceremony was held at Anna's parish church. Two bridesmaids and Lily preceded her down the aisle. Lily wore her hair up for the first time, and a little makeup, and suddenly looked older. She was very calm. Bob took Marcus's hand as she passed their pew.

Anna looked radiant as her older brother Franco walked her to the altar. Her dress was simple but elegant and she held her large bouquet of flowers strategically over her stomach.

Bob and Marcus sat with Jason.

"Where's Joel?" Marcus whispered.

Jason sighed. "Gone."

"Gone? Gone where?"

"Just gone. He said he wasn't ready for anything serious."

"Oh, Jason. I'm sorry."

He had to smile. "So am I. By the way," Jason said, lowering his voice and bending toward Marcus. "I just heard from Detective Sanchez. Emma was in a traffic accident last night."

"Was she hurt?" Marcus felt a bit of panic, although he wasn't sure why.

"Yes. She's in the hospital."

Marcus closed his eyes.

The wedding reception was a luncheon at the La Jolla Country Club; Alejandro's firm was a client. It, too, was simple but tasteful.

Lily wanted to join the other single girls to see if she could catch the bouquet, but Bob stopped her.

"Sweet pea, no, you're too young," he said.

That night, they ordered pizza at home with Rick and Jay, who had moved in together in a little apartment in Hillcrest. Lily went to sleep early, and the boys said they were going dancing.

"Ah, the young," Marcus said.

Bob showered while Marcus lingered in the living room. He looked at a photo on the fireplace mantle. It showed Bob on the grass in the backyard with their old retriever, Oscar, and Lily just after her fifth birthday. It was a favorite photo: Bob was cuddling Lily and Oscar was licking her face. Marcus remembered how Oscar and Lily had instantly bonded and smiled to himself.

Next to it was another photo he loved, of all three of them playing in the snow in Connecticut. They had flown back for the wedding of Bob's first cousin in Danbury, his home town. Standing off to the side were Jake and Ruth, beaming. Marcus couldn't remember which of Bob's cousins had taken the picture.

Lily had never seen snow and looked at it with wonder.

77

A month later, the local news announced that Rudd Martin had pleaded guilty to second-degree murder; there would be no trial. The DA announced that after "an exhaustive investigation" there was "insufficient evidence" to charge Emma Baker with any crime. The story said she was recovering from serious injuries from a car crash and was convalescing "at an undisclosed location."

Her house in La Jolla was up for sale, the story continued, and she had resigned from UCSD. From her deceased husband she had inherited "over ten million dollars."

❧❧❧❧

Acknowledgments

Heartfelt thanks to the indispensable editor Priscilla Long, to Ana Cara, Sandra Zagarell, and Carter McAdams, for reading drafts, and once again to A.D. Reed of Pisgah Press.

This is a work of fiction. Aside from any brief mentions of public figures, no true events or real individuals are depicted.

ABOUT THE AUTHOR

H. N. Hirsch was born in Chicago and educated at the University of Michigan and at Princeton. A political scientist by training, he has been on the faculties of Harvard, the University of California-San Diego, Macalester College, and Oberlin, where he served as Dean of the Faculty and is now the Erwin N. Griswold Professor of Politics Emeritus. He is the author of *The Enigma of Felix Frankfurter* ("brilliant and sure to be controversial"—*The New York Times*), *A Theory of Liberty*, and the memoir *Office Hours* ("well crafted and wistful"—Kirkus), and numerous articles on law, politics, and constitutional questions.

About Pisgah Press

Pisgah Press was established in 2011 in Asheville, NC to publish works of quality offering original ideas and insight into the human condition and the world around us. If you support the old-fashioned tradition of publishing for the pleasure of the reader and the benefit of the author, please encourage your friends and colleagues to order directly from the publisher at www.PisgahPress.com. For more information about Pisgah Press books, contact us at pisgahpress@gmail.com.

Also available from Pisgah Press

Gabriel's Songbook   Michael Amos Cody
$17.95   FINALIST, FEATHERED QUILL BOOK AWARD, FICTION, 2021
A Twilight Reel
$17.95   GOLD MEDALIST, FEATHERED QUILL BOOK AWARD, SHORT STORIES, 2021

Letters of the Lost Children: Japan—WWII   Reinhold C. Ferster
$37.95   & Jan Atchley Bevan

Musical Morphine: Transforming Pain One Note at a Time   Robin Russell Gaiser
$17.95   FINALIST, USA BOOK AWARDS, 2017
Open for Lunch
$17.95

Fault Line   THE BOB & MARCUS MYSTERY SERIES   H.N. Hirsch
22.95
Shade
22.95
Rain
22.95

The Last of the Swindlers   Peter Loewer
$17.95

Homo Sapiens: A Violent Gene?   Mort Malkin
$22.95

Reed's Homophones: A Comprehensive Book of Sound-alike Words   A.D. Reed
$17.95

Swords in their Hands: George Washington and the Newburgh Conspiracy   Dave Richards
$24.95   FINALIST, USA BOOK AWARDS, HISTORY, 2014

Port City   Eliot Ssefrin
$27.95 hardcover / $19.95 paper

Trang Sen: A Novel of Vietnam   Sarah-Ann Smith
$19.50

Deadly Dancing   THE RICK RYDER MYSTERY SERIES   RF Wilson
$15.95
Killer Weed
$14.95
The Pot Professor
$17.95
Murder on the Rocks
$22.95

To order:

P

Pisgah Press, LLC
PO Box 9663, Asheville, NC 28815
www.pisgahpress.com

www.ingramcontent.com/pod-product-compliance
Lightning Source LLC
Jackson TN
JSHW081941020725
87093JS00015B/101